Sexcapades & Champagne

Sexcapades & Champagne

Lexa James

Published 2012 by HumorOutcasts Press
Printed in the United States of America

ISBN 0-615-67727-4
EAN-13 978-061567727-9

Contents

Prelude

Virginity? Eh...

I gave "it" up at fourteen. Young I know, but it was one of those times when I had done everything else with my then boyfriend, including sucking peanut butter off his cock. And it was just time. However, on reflection maybe the peanut butter should've come after. Anyway, we had met at a friend's house while playing "Seven Minutes in Heaven". After it was on with his king dong. I mean seriously he was hung and I was so gorgeous then. I remember the song "I'm Fucking You Tonight" was playing as I opened my thighs on his ratty futon. I'd say it lasted maybe five minutes? And like that, virginity gone and on to the next.

I was the first in my circle at school to lose my "it", and that made me feel empowered. And the more I did "it" and the more virgins I bedded, the stronger I felt. There was Thomas whose little brother is probably still scarred trying to figure out what his older siblings face was doing between my legs. Because let's face it most men still don't understand it. Matt who was the hottest senior in my high school. I mean there mere sight of him had most of the clits in school standing on end, probably a few hard cocks too. I owned him on his waterbed to "Peaches and Cream". We also worked the shocks on the back of his pick-up after football games. To this day he's the only blonde man I've ever fucked that I can remember.

Humor, freaks, orgasms and booze. Welcome to my trip down my sexual memory lane... and then some.

Ass Backwards

How does a girl remember her first time being sodomized? The word for that would be fondly, if I wasn't too smashed from plastic bottle vodka and filled with the adrenaline of reckless dares in my high school years to remember anything.

I had a thing for "bad boys". It was much like my DJ fetish. The thing with "bad boys" is they are often retarded and do things ass backwards. (Pun intended)

I tend to have a thing for everything at some point. Most people think it's because I'm just too fickle, indecisive, or even stubborn. I just like to think I would prefer variety over commitment. It's easy to become another mold of what every other family in America has become. Get married, raise spawns of Satan that will run around the apartment complex screaming "Bang! Bang!" and eventually get rid of every piece of what you were, to just maintain yourselves slightly above the "People of Walmart" middle-America cusp. That isn't me now, nor do I think it will ever be me. It's not that I don't want to get married one day, it's just that I'm too far into my bad boy phase to even contemplate anything more than living in the now.

But even though they are what I like to classify as "Bad Boys," Ryan just might have joined the ranks of a whole new category I have labeled, "Not fit for life."

You see, Ryan was one of the bad boys, but in the stupidest of ways. Always drunk during the day and stoned at night--the reverse of any intelligent human that has discovered the great benefits of alcohol and drug use. But we all make mistakes in high school. Most can be forgotten or aborted. Not Ryan though. Ryan seemed to be the product of a pregnancy that the mother must have not known about until 6 months in, and she continued to drink and party hard up until that point. Then if you took that, and bred it with the IQ of something from The Hills Have Eyes, but with the sex appeal of an English rock star, that was him.

We had "dated" for a few months which while in my high school years simply meant pounding vodka from plastic bottles, beer pong with hard cider and fucking in his chain smoking mother's bed. She never seemed to mind. She was even sweet enough to cover me up after Ryan would defile me while I was passed out on her living room floor.

Oh, what it meant to be in love when you were young, dumb, and willing to be filled with cum. I was pretty much willing to try everything once in my later teenage years, and if I wasn't willing to try it at first there was definitely a price or a specific amount of alcohol that could push me towards proceeding with the idea.

I remember specifically there was one night we were over at a friend's house while her parents were out of town and besides the teenage drunkenness, this was about as John Hughes as it got. I'm not sure how but I ended up face down on the floor of my friend's room, anal cavity full of baby oil, insisting to Ryan he was drunk and it didn't work that way. I'm pretty sure though that it was somewhere between the countless jello shots, and maybe even some of the cough syrup I chugged on a dare that might have contributed to that comprising situation.

One might ask if it was enjoyable? I don't remember. Nor do I really care to recall it at this point in my life. Especially after countless enjoyable experiences when it came to anal sex.

But as I was with my virginity, I was the first in my class to earn the anal sex slut point.

The Date with His Sister

"What the fuck happened last night?" Is a question I find myself asking a little too often anymore.

It's 8 a.m. and once again I'm doing the walk of shame for my dogs. Damn their judging eyes. What the hell ever. It's Sunday and as soon as I peel off last night's dress that screams "slut", I'm going to bed.

Ford. Another product of the lovely Los Angeles online dating scene. He kept well in my trend of men a decade older than myself, and he downed a martini so fast it'd lead you to believe he was the one lowering his standards for this meeting. He dressed well and spoke with distinction despite his obvious alcoholism.

We ordered dinner and the vodka flowed and flowed, allowing for some pretty great conversation although it was a bit slurred. What was supposed to be a quick bite and cocktails turned into four hours of flirting and the exchange of life stories. I would say it was lovely, if it was not for the fact he kept texting under the table. I mean doing it on occasion is fine, I had done it earlier to cancel my second date of the evening, but come on.

So, I asked him as politely as I could on three martinis, who he was texting. "Oh, just my sister," he replied. At first, I was like "Oh how sweet," until I hit my fourth martini, and he hit his 400th text. So, I moved onto the fifth to keep the booze flowing at the same rate of Ford's data plan and the big red flag slapping me in my face. All in all, this date with him and his sister was going well. We did after all shut down the restaurant and in keeping with my pursuit of alcohol I suggested we get a room and raid the mini-bar. I knew what this implied and he was up for it.

Awe, the Hilton Hotel and its crappy "romance" package of shitty strawberries and cheap champagne. But most importantly a clean bathroom to wash away the sins I was about to commit that night and the next morning. I quickly pop the bottle while surprise, surprise he's texting his sister. At this point the red flag is tickling my clit, so I start firing. Are you married? Is that really your sister? Do have a girlfriend? But he stuck to his story word for word like he practiced in his car on the way to dinner. So, what the hell. I gave myself to him, with his spray tan and shaved chest.

He performed like the crappy American car I'm sure he was named after. Then he went right back to texting his "sister" leaving me at home six hours later with two judgmental dogs eyeing me and a Lifetime movie.

Fucking Hollywood Blvd

The ancient voice on my modern smart phone chimed with excitement as it let me know, 'You've Got Mail.' Cliché, I know. But I've always been a fan of the silliness of it all. And I'm such a sucker for retro technology.

I opened the unread message to find it from a guy I met via online dating named Matt. The beautiful thing about online dating in Los Angeles is that even if the date sucks, there's always plenty of alcohol in abundance which can sometimes lead to the occasional, 'Well, I wasn't planning on having C minus sex last night. although I have to give the spontaneity an A.'

Matt was harder than his dick could ever get. Ripped abs of pure pleasure, all ruined with the irony of him holding a dead fish he had caught on some weekend at some lake no one really could give two shits about.

You might be thinking this seems a bit harsh to say, especially straight off the bat without giving Matt any redeeming qualities. And that's honestly because there weren't any redeeming qualities. I can usually spot at least a few great things in people, even with my ridiculously high expectations. But with Matt, I had nothing of the positive sort cross my mind once.

The details of the email asked about meeting up again. I thought, "A repeat performance? Please.. you barely made it through the first" But of course I sent him something quite more diplomatic but with the same touch to it.

Another ding, and my phone was vibrating with a new message.

Really? Did he not get the hint in the last message? Alright, time to be a little more aggressive.

How clingy can you really be, Matt? You are thirty-two years old and still live in the valley with a roommate. Failure is written all over you. Plus, you fuck like the dead fish in your profile picture. There is no way in hell this is happening again. EVER.

Unfortunately, I am far too easily persuaded by the thought of wine and food for which I might have to at least give him some credit in that he could pick up on that after our first disaster of a night. So I met him at Cobras & Matadors on Hollywood Boulevard for a retake. First impressions are something special, especially if I'm going to be spending the next hour staring at you from across the table. And as a future reference to all guys out there, if you show up looking like the creepy camera guy from *Girls Gone Wild*, or any member of *Jersey Shore*, you won't get very far.

The wine was great even with a conversation lacking any and all intelligence. It really made sitting across from this thirty-two year old with a roommate and the mentality of an alcohol-retarded frat boy somewhat bearable.

If you asked me what we talked about that night, I couldn't tell you. I really wasn't paying attention. I was drinking. But I was quickly able to cut the cord on this tedious part of the night by ordering a second bottle of wine, on his tab of course. He was more than happy to pay for a pricey bottle of wine the first time around, but not the second. And if I had it my way, he would have paid for a third and fourth bottle as well.

He quickly grabbed the check as the second bottle came, so he wouldn't be forced into paying for more alcohol of mine. But two bottles of some high class booze were more than enough to get me staggering to the car without a care in the world. As I fumbled with my keys getting ready to drunkenly drive my way back home, he slammed me up against the car and started kissing the back of my neck.

The aggressive factor he brought to it had me super wet, but then I had to remind myself it was him doing it... instant lady boner killer. He did something for himself that the wine could never do. He got hotter.

The way I could feel his rock hard cock through his jeans bulging onto my leg, it went from no interest to too much instantly. Homeless people stopped and stared, almost like our own private audience. He took my keys without missing a beat on my lips, and opened the door. In a swift and passionate motion he shoved me in the backseat, and the fuck was on.

This is probably one of the only times you will hear me say I am so happy to drive an SUV. Otherwise, this wouldn't have happened. He had me face down, ass up across the backseat, while he quickly forced his fingers into me. It felt so wrong, but so good. The fingers quickly turned into full on sex as he unzipped his pants, and stuck his dick through the hole and straight into me. It slid in with perfection.

There wasn't much of a size difference between his fingers and his cock, but I wasn't in a mood to care. And a quick ten minutes later he was wiping himself off onto a dirty shirt he found in my car. Twenty minutes after that? I was washing a combination of slut and shame off of myself.

As I lay down after my shower, my phone chimed again..a cringe-worthy, **ominous** chime. It's him, again. What the hell.

Fuck. Now I find myself in need of a restraining order.

Bartending & Biker Boss

There was a two year stretch during my college years when I had become heavily obsessed with biking. Not the normal biking with fixies or fancy BMX tricks, but the extravagant lifestyle of those who travel in biker gangs. Even though I grew up pretty much strapped on to the backseat of my stepdad's motorcycle, it hadn't really struck this magnitude of a fascination until as of late. While I was on a college student budget of top Ramen and stealing WIFI from the nearest Starbucks, it still entertained me to daydream for hours on end about hitting the open road, shredded leather barely covering my breasts, and the 80 mile-per-hour wind blowing through my hair.

But even at the lowest income of my life, I would still pull enough strings to make a trip to Sturgis, South Dakota for the annual bike rally they would hold. Now if you aren't quite sure what a bike rally is, it's where thousands upon thousands of college students, bikers, and half-naked women would come to this Podunk town and turn it into something memorable. And it wasn't just like they were all locals, coming from the surrounding states across the borders. Most of these people would fly, or ride in from all ends of the nation.

And it wasn't just people who were into bikes that would show up. Thousands of college kids would meet up in this small town in the Black Hills for a week of drunken debauchery, concerts, and of course, naked girls. Me being the 23-year-old university student I was at the time, the money invested in the trip out there was well worth the cost of what I would get out of going there.

And it really did become an investment taking the annual trip out there. I needed some extra money for this shitty education I had been receiving, and somehow, ending up in the middle of this 14-day straight rager did more than break even on the trip expense. Having a few friends who lived in town, I was able to not only have a free place to crash, but also able to pick up a few bar-tending gigs for the duration of the trip.

The shenanigans in this hick town begin in the month of August. Why of all months they chose the one that makes this place becomes a walking sauna is far beyond my comprehension. But I guess the best part about the heat from a guy's perspective is that Wet T-Shirt Contests are no longer an option for us females, but become rather mandatory if we wish to stay cool.

My friend's Kristin and Bob own a 12-bedroom house out there, and were more than happy letting me cozy up in one of the rooms for the two weeks. They often would rent out extra rooms to some of the bikers that come in to town to make a bit of extra cash on the side. And they would even let me help out around the house a couple days a week to split some of that extra money with me. For being broke during the rest of the year, this trip really helped me pay for next semester's expenses in full.

I had just arrived, and I could already smell the fried food and shame covering the land like the thick smog of downtown Los Angeles. The sound of ZZ Top and Kid Rock was creating a chaotic noise outside their house as the bikers started rolling in. First a couple here and there, almost looking like they wandered into the wrong part of town. Then, 20 at a time…30…until finally it was a solid stream and standstill of bikers flooding the road ways. This was my favorite part to watch of all the events. Not because they were arriving, rowdy and ready to party. But for that pure chance that one of them would accidentally hit another's bike, and start the best street brawl you will ever witness.

I have one day before I start my bartending gig down the street. And that means I frankly only have one day to relax, get a bit settled in, and get completely wasted with all these freaks. After having a drink, or two, maybe three, I decided it was time to set forth into town and check out all the shops. With my great buzz going on, I even considered the possibility of getting a trashy and matching tattoo with one of the biker chicks, for the hell of it.

But with the heat pulsating from the pavement onto my bronzed skin, I needed to find cover and fast before I fainted from my drunken dehydration and got trampled to death by this ruthless and reckless crowd. The air I was breathing in was nothing more than hot man breath, the kind you get from the gross guy at the club who tries to grind on you during another moderately successful Top 40 track. But despite the generalization of the grunge of the crowd, there were men and women here who represented every walk of life. True Hells Angels. They were doctors, lawyers, politicians, and even just your average and typical American family. It was quite a show to see a diversity of this magnitude when it is often considered a white trash stereotype. And growing up on the backseat of my stepdad's bike made me feel quite at home amongst strangers.

I ran and hid in the nearest bar I could find, and ordered up a tall one. I drank it slowly, trying to cool off my skin, and even struck up a conversation with a few lovely fellas over a game of darts. It was definitely, the best way to spend the afternoon. As the sun started to set, I was going to make my way back to the house by foot, but one of the guys I had been talking to, and rather enjoying his company, offered to drive me back if I'd stay and hang another hour.

We talked about the stuff small talk folks find entertaining--celebrity gossip, NASCAR (which I knew nothing of at the time), and the weather. It didn't bother me one bit to drop my IQ to his level for a few free drinks and some companionship. But it did bother me at the end of the night when he dropped me off, and I realized I never once actually asked his name. Normally, in a small town that wouldn't be a problem, but when the population of the town easily triples overnight, finding John Doe might be trickier than posed. Oh well.

The next day I woke to a horrifying smell of breakfast, B.O., and the overuse of Axe body spray. This party had officially started. I went downstairs in my cute lingerie to find dozens of biker dudes feasting on sausage, omelettes, fresh squeezed orange juice and of course, beer. I had to carefully position myself to reach over them and get some breakfast to take back to my room, but these old pervs still managed to find a way to cop a feel on my goods. Well, it wasn't the first time that's happened, and I guess walking into a room full of men and wearing nothing, I couldn't expect less than that.

When you're exotic and young in the middle of a dominantly white crowd in middle America, you tend to attract a lot of attention just walking down the street. And with my Daisy Dukes, leather and gold cowboy boots with one of those cute tied up midriff tops, the attention I received easily multiplied tenfold. I made sure that before I arrived here, I mastered the perfect shade of bronze on my skin. It really wasn't that hard to do when I was managing a tanning salon next door to my university. The heat here was still too intense to make a cute hair style actually stay, so throwing it up in my signature messy bun was going to have to do on this one. I looked pretty amazing, and this really helped for my first day on the job.

I walked into the bar and I was immediately struck with an intimidating and ominous feeling hovering over me by all the local girls I was about to work with. It's not that I wasn't comparable to them, because my looks were far superior to theirs, but it was the simple fact that they knew the turf, for lack of better wording. The owner of the bar, who was a 30-something, tall, dark and handsome type, brought us all in to the back room, around a makeshift table made out of cinder blocks and wood, with milk crates as chairs. We sat for the next hour discussing basic rules and guidelines, and even just shooting the shit with one another. It was probably the best thing that could happen because by the end of that pow-wow, I had become pretty much best friends with each of the girls.

I got put in charge of running the outdoor bar, which was amazing because I was out there solo. This meant more take-home tips for me at the end of the night, which pleased my wallet. Even though I was new, and everyone knew I was temporary, the first two days I already had some repeaters who made sure to let me know that I gave them the best service they had ever gotten in this establishment. I blushed with joy, knowing that those were the guys who would come back every night till I left town just to buy one beer and leave me a large tip. Maybe a large tip in even in more than one way too.

But I'm a natural flirt, and I do it so effortlessly that I don't even notice at this point anymore. It's day three of working here, and my hands are starting to blister from opening so many beers. Each day I have worked has been a long, tiresome 12-hour shift. There's no time to party when you're working 11am – 11pm, which is unfortunate because some of these characters who have come through my shift have been just my type.

I just started my shift when the owner Jay came down and sat at the bar. His sunglasses were on, almost as if he was trying to hide the worst hangover of his life. Lit cigarette in his mouth, and asks me in a musky sort of way for a "Red Beer." If I wasn't a broke college student

I may have never known what that actually meant. In a nutshell, it is a poor man's Bloody Mary. You take a Bud Light and top it with a bit of tomato juice. Sounds absolutely disgusting, but I can attest that it is indeed a miracle worker.

As he sipped the drink, and the sting of last night slowly wore off him, he asked me if I wanted to take a ride with him through the hills later today. I tell him, "I'd love to, but I'm here till close." He gave me this unamused look and belches, '"Lexa, I'm the boss. If I say let's go for a ride, you best bet your shift is covered." It was a bit off putting to hear that from someone not only of authority, but from this part of the world. I wasn't sure if going for a ride meant sex or if he was going to murder me and leave me in the hills at this point. But his rugged charm, and working man good looks had me surrendering with a big, "Yes, I'll be there then."

The two o'clock hour rolled around rather quickly when I heard the purring of his shiny, chromed out bike roll up to the side of the bar. I hung up my bartending apron and ran out the door and sat comfortably on the back of his bike. I'm not one to fall in love with nature, especially because I love the busy aspect of the city life, but the scenery out here in South Dakota was something truly to be cherished. The wind was blowing my hair just as I had often daydreamed about during the college semesters to get me through days of mundane lectures. The scent of dirt and pine reminded me of all the times I went camping in the summer as a kid with the local youth groups. The reality I was living was better than any production a cliché Hollywood film could ever produce.

This was a small slice of heaven on Earth, and it was actually happening to me in front of my own eyes!

After a good 20-minute drive or so up the windiest of roads, we stopped off in a little town that resembled the set of an old western flick. The roads were made of dirt, and that dirt pretty much covered everything in that town. For a few seconds, I actually thought it was a secret ghost town that he might have been taking me to. We got off the bike, and he led the way to this rustic tavern. The inside of the tavern was just like an old saloon. Stale, dirty air filled my nostrils along with the mustiness of stale, dirty, town folks. But it was nothing less than what I would expect based on my brief fascination with westerns years back. This was seemingly perfect, even as gross as it was.

He stepped up to the bar and ordered four oyster shooters and two beers to chase them down with. They were surprisingly delicious. And I started to get the impression that he was trying to flirt with me. But I may have been mistaking his silence for something quite different, seeing as he had been a man of few words up to this point.

As we finished up our drinks, he urged for us to get a move on. We headed back out and onto the bike. As we rode on, I got this tingly feeling inside like I was starting to feel something for him--almost a strange crush. We rode on for a good five hours before starting to make our way back to the rally. It was a soul-moving experience to just ride with no expectations, motivation, or desires. It felt like I had found my quaint little piece of serenity where I had least expected it.

He pulled up and parked at the bar, just where he had picked me up. The sarcasm in me was screaming, "This isn't awkward at all," as the other girls gave me strange looks. I've gotten those looks before when favoritism had entered the picture, though at least this time it's only a couple of weeks that I have to endure it, and not some undetermined period of time.

Jay told me to pay no attention to them, and gave them a shooing signal to get back to their duties. I told him it was getting late, and that I needed to head home. He may come across as an asshole with his lack of words, and very blunt ones when he does choose to speak, but he has this strangely large heart. He offered repeatedly to give me a ride home, but I just couldn't take that after spending the whole day with him and then having to spend all of the next day with the girls at the bar. I told him it was a nice night out and that I'd rather walk since it was only a half mile up the road. So he took up the offer and said, "That's ok, I'll walk with you." Well, I couldn't really fight that one off now can I.

He came in briefly to get a glass of water. But I knew the game, and I knew where this is heading. It worked the same with cups of coffee, having a smoke, and it being too cold outside. I brought him downstairs to my room because I didn't want to wake the barely sleeping and still drunk household of testosterone. I let him know that I was tired and I was ready to go to bed quite soon. I lay down and he took the opportunity to join me. Even though he smelled strongly of cigarette smoke and the day's ride, I couldn't help but have the tingles start up again in my stomach. I thought to myself, "Guess I'll just wash the sheets tomorrow to get the stink out," as I rolled over onto his chest.

He took his hand to the bottom of my chin, and guided me up past his scratchy five o'clock shadow and straight to his lips. While this was moving too fast in a sense, it was quite pleasant to get straight to the point for once especially when I still have a 12-hour shift in less than 10 hours. While this might seem like it was still far enough away to get freaky and get some shut eye, there's just something about me when it comes to both sex and my beauty rest. I like them both long and fulfilling.

My shirt had come up a little on the side, exposing more of my midriff than it previously had. He took his hand and slid it down my curves and made his way into my pants. Slowly, and with deep penetration, he slid his fingers in and out of me. It's one thing to be fingered by a guy during a sloppy and drunken one night stand, but to have a real man, with working hands touch you, is a truly magical experience.

My shorts quickly became soaked with pure ecstasy as he started using his other hand to take them off the rest of the way. I could not believe how quickly he had me gasping for air! I was right on the verge of coming when he slid out his fingers and dragged them down across my leg to change up the position. He licked me off his fingers and got on top of me. He slowly kissed my body down each and every curve until he found a sweet spot to nibble on. He made his way past my hips and down to my vagina, where he kissed it sweetly and passionately inserted his tongue ever so slightly into me.

He then took his hand and thrust his fingers into me, as he used his tongue to playfully massage my clit. He continued doing this for quite some time till I finally let it all go and came all over his face. He licked all of it up, like every man should. Then he lays next to me in bed, and fell asleep with his arm around my waist.

My mind was racing at a thousand miles per hour at this point. We didn't even have sex which first of all was completely mind blowing, and weird. Furthermore, I didn't even go down on him, nor did he make any attempt to make me try to do so. And lastly, I just hooked up with my boss! What the hell was I thinking? But instead of him taking off like a bandit after getting what he came for, he completely passed out next to me with his arm around my waist holding me in a cuddling fashion, and spooning my right side. This is so not typical, especially for a man that is roughly six feet of scruffy, rugged handsomeness.

My alarm went off at 10am, and Jay was already gone. He must have crept out at some point this morning to go and unlock the bar for some of the girls. I wasn't going to think too much about that. Really, I wasn't going to think about it at all. I had roughly 10 days left here, and I was just going to pretend that I had never brought him home last night and that it was all just a dream and that I am going to just work out the remainder of my days and move on back to my good ole college town. But I can't keep the thought running through my mind, "What the hell did you do

As I get up and get going for my shift at the bar, I don't even stop to eat the breakfast my friends had prepared especially for me. Instead, I bolt out the door in a hurry to just get this day started, and over with as soon as possible. I get to the bar, and the girls are treating me like nothing happened. Ok, this is cool. I can handle this. We all laugh, joke, and even take a few shots throughout the day. As the day starts to wind up, I count my tips and see that I had made almost $400 in tips just from the evening alone. For a college student, that is a great day when when it comes to finances!

I got off work, and started walking down the starlit trail, back to my friends' house. Off in the distance I heard the humming of a motorcycle making its way towards me. As it got closer, I realized that it was Jay, and that he was once again here to hook up. But in my heart, I just couldn't do it. I kept walking at the same pace, hoping to make it to the house before he could catch up, but I wasn't so lucky. He slowed down next to me and asked if I wanted a lift the rest of the way. There was a part of me that wanted to giggle and say "sure", but the other part of me just wanted a clean break from this all. I really enjoyed hooking up, but that was really all I enjoyed. And it wasn't fair to lead him on with a two-week fling, when I probably wouldn't be coming back the next year after graduating.

I had to be honest and blunt. He was a man who stayed true to "telling it like it is," so he shouldn't be too put off if I leveled with him. "Jay, I really enjoyed last night, but it's just not something I can get into at this moment in time." He respected it, and still offered to drive me the rest of the way with no strings attached. I politely declined, and he made his way back the opposite way of which I came from. That seemed to go smoothly. But knowing my luck, just a little too smooth.

The next day at the bar around closing, he was waiting outside for me to give me a ride. Any other girl would appreciate the gesture of someone being so romantic, but to me it wasn't only professionally inappropriate but downright creepy. I told him once again that I was not interested in hooking up for those reasons, and he apologized and rode off. I couldn't tell if I was being mean or not at this point, but I stood by my honesty on this one.

I may have made a mistake even letting him take things that far that night in my room, but it's still something I wouldn't change. And throughout the remainder of my trip he still asked every night after work if I wanted a ride home. His desperation was cute at first, but during my final days I was happy when my friends were giving me the ride to the airport to go home, and not him.

When I finally got situated on the plane, I opened a small envelope I got from Jay as my final payout with tips included. I started counting through it, expecting him to cheap me out for not putting out. Instead, I was more than thrilled to find well over $5,000 in there from tips alone. Needless to say I spent the rest of the plane trip guarding that envelope with my life. I don't think there has ever been a moment in time where a college student has had as much money as I did in my bank account after a trip to South Dakota.

City of Sin & Skin

Let's face it, every person on the planet or at least within the United States. has had a dirty Las Vegas fantasy. And if they haven't had the fantasy, it's more than likely because they've already lived it and experienced what the scandalous city has to offer. And for one second if you tried to prove me wrong, I would call you a liar and ask what you were trying to hide or what went down on your last visit there.

There really isn't much to love about this adult-rated city, but I have been able to accept there are five things it has to offer that I will always cherish. First and foremost, it is a beautiful city in the middle of the desert. The buildings tower over the strip, and each hotel brings something different to the plate. You can start at the front of the strip at MGM Grand, with their luscious wild life vibe, and take a brisk walk across the street and feel like you're in New York. A short distance later, you can visit Rome, Paris, or pretend you are rich and live it up at the more luxurious settings the town has to offer.

Secondly, I love this town because it doesn't judge. You can be on the verge of pushing daisies or underage with a fake ID, and debauchery is always more than welcome for the right price. Trashy pool parties during the day with sexy, shirtless and oiled up DJ's? Yes please! Overpriced fruity cocktails? Count me in especially when there is a desperate guy more than willing to pay. This also ties into my third reason as to why I love Vegas, which is the fact there is no sense of time in this city. Ever walk into a casino and realize there are no clocks on the wall? They want you to get lost in there, lose track of time, and your money. Maybe even lose some of your dignity if the price is right. But I digress.

My fourth reason why I love this city are the escorts. I love to watch them hard at work and working the pockets of old men and drunk fraternity guys.

And the last reason to love Vegas is quite obvious: the sexual possibilities are endless. You can have a romantic getaway with a lover, or enjoy a casual fling with a stranger. But that's just the tip of that sexy iceberg. The places you can hook up at are endless. There are so many individuals visiting Vegas on a daily basis that law enforcement is slim to none. While it's not quite my style, I have watched countless individuals drunkenly go at it on the strip more times than I feel comfortable counting.

It was a hot day, like any day in this sin city. I was poolside in my golden bikini at the Mandalay Bay Hotel, looking almost like a goddess with my sun-kissed skin oiled up with liquid glitter. I was already a couple drinks in to my suntan routine when I was overcome with a dark, but warm shadow. I look up to see a tall man, roughly six feet tall and abs of steel that showed the five o'clock shadow of a happy trail. And that happy trail was definitely leading to a happy place for me, whether he knew it or not.

He was a bit bold, and I liked that. He handed me another one of those strawberry paradise drinks I had been sipping and he introduced himself to me as, "Nicholas". In my hazy drunk, he could have told me his name was, "Hey girl, let's go up to my room and get a bit freaky," and I would have more than been happy to oblige. We chatted for a bit over the deafening and terrible house music blasting in the background long enough for me to get both his room and cell numbers. As he drifted away, I assumed the position to continue my regime of tanning before a long night out on the town.

As the sun began its descent to the other side of the world, I decided it was time to head back to the room and get in a quick power nap before an evening of debauchery and shenanigans. As I drifted off to sleep, I was abruptly awakened, but pleasantly, to the sound of my cell phone ringing. It was Nicholas asking if I wanted to meet up with him and his friends for a couple of drinks down at the hotel bar in an hour. My answer? "Of course."

I got up and showered. The hot water gave a bit of a sting to my borderline sunburnt skin, but a little bit of aloe lotion would fix that up quite nicely. I quickly dried off and threw my towel to the ground as I ran across the room to my suitcase. I quickly pulled out my little black dress, which has gotten me laid more often than I can recall. As a solid B-Cup, there aren't many times I get the chance to show them off with such sass. The dress was sexy, stunning, yet classy. Now, all I needed to do was fix up my hair and layer on a thick but natural layer of makeup and I was set to jet downstairs.

I was barely down on the casino floor, when my six-inch stripper heels already started to take their toll. But hey, hooker heels, fake lashes and nude lip gloss is what Vegas is all about, right? The moment I met up with

Nicholas and his friends, they begged me to join in a few rounds of shots even though they were two rounds ahead of me already. Now, I hate shots. But I am not one to turn down one... two... or three especially when they're free.

I should have mentioned before this that I was on this Vegas trip with my friends, but up until this point they were off sightseeing and doing their own thing-- things that I was highly uninterested in. But when it came to me gossiping like a giddy and boy-crazed school girl, they just had to meet up with me to see what this Nicholas guy was all about.

As we downed a few more shots, my friends nudged me with dissatisfaction and annoyance that most girls give to their partners when they ignore them for the Super Bowl. So I gave Nicholas a little peck and we made our way off to a night of club hopping with underdressed girls, $1,000 bottle service and sweaty guys in yesterday's bad fashion. But I can't complain too much because tonight I am one of those underdressed girls and I am more wasted than any other time I spent in this city.

My girlfriends and I were spinning under the disco lights, a sea of lasers beamed above us. The strobe disoriented us. We were getting pretty rowdy to some over remixed version of *Show Me Love* when I come to a stop on the dance floor and saw Nicholas across the room. It was almost like fate or rather, a boozed up version of destiny. Before he came over to meet us, I let my friends know I am going to get a new drink and use the ladies room. I mean, that's a probable excuse for getting lost in a club for an hour, right?

I grabbed his hand as I chugged another shot, and we ran across the congested strip and back down to the Mandalay. We barely made it out of the elevator before his hands were already up my dress and down my black lace panties. As we tumbled our way across the wall of the hallway I frantically searched my bra for the room key. But once I found it, it seemed to take an eternity between the aggressive make out session going on, and getting the key in the door and opened. But once that hotel swung open with full force, it was on.

The motion of him picking me up and me jumping up to wrap my legs around his chiseled torso happened with swift accuracy. He grabbed my hair and thrust me into the mirror closet door, leaving a nice crack running down the entire thing from where my back had impacted it. My dress was so short, it didn't have to come off for him to make his way down to where I wanted him. Hell, even my undies didn't have to come off either as he pinned me up against the wall. Each thrust made the framed artwork on the wall shake and shift, until one by one they made their descent, crashing and shattering on the floor. We fucked like animals. On the desk, under the desk, on the bed, pressed up against the window baring it all to the strip. If there was not some sort of Karma Sutra in the Hotel book already, we wrote it that night.

We made our way back onto the bed, and he thrust inside of me and let his man juice fill the condom. Normally, I wasn't one to condone this, but it is Vegas. So a great

Vegas story wouldn't be complete without something as risque. He collapsed next to me, and longingly stared into my eyes as we both let out the tiniest of giggles. What do we do next?

Our friends were expecting us to be somewhere, and I had already felt my phone vibrate a couple times on the bed while we tossed ourselves about the room. I sprung up off the bed and shifted down my dress to inspect it for any love stains. When I saw that I was spotless, I fixed up my hair with a quick messy bun and cleaned up my make up ever so slightly. The best part about fake eyelashes is once they're on, they don't come off for quite some time.

We walked towards the elevator laughing hysterically at what just happened. On the way out of the casino we grabbed another shot of tequila and a bottle of water to quench our thirst as we sprang back across the strip to the same club where we ditched our friends.

It was funny that when I got back into the club and found them, they hadn't even moved an inch from their snug little spot on the middle of the dance floor. Hell, my friends didn't even notice I was missing and to this day, they still don't know I was missing. I was able to play it off to them that the hotel was a mess because someone must have robbed us. I also made some great excuse about the hotel charged us for it until they could solve the case, then we would get reimbursed. The best thing about my friends is that a week after the Vegas trip, they had already forgotten about what a mess the hotel had become that night. And the best part about Vegas? I sure will never forget what a hot mess it makes me time and time again.

Crooked Inches & Cash Drawers

I've always been one to hang out primarily with guys, but that need to have only guys as friends grew greater when they all started coming out of the closet towards the end of high school. Having a gay guy as a friend is like having all the fun, boy giggling, and fashion advising that a girl can offer minus the one week a month she goes into melt down mode when Aunt Flow comes to town.

So it should come as no surprise that in certain circles, I am what is considered to be a "fag hag". I actually prefer to think of myself as "The Queer Queen". Being the Queer Queen had become my one of my greatest accomplishments and at the same time one of my greatest burdens.

It happens more often or not when I am out on the town with "my gays" that the men I fuck are going to be the ones secure enough in their manhood to be at a gay bar. Be it joke or truth, one of my talents is finding the one straight cock in the orgy of gay ones. And there's no better place to look than in the city I call my second home, West Hollywood.

It started off as just a causal night of drinking overpriced cocktails made with cheap liquor and far too much filler; gossip about dick size and sodomy, (two things I'm well versed in) at this dimly lit lounge. If you've been to one bar in Hollywood, or any of the surrounding areas, that pretty much sums up every bar, at least from my experience. While some may be a bit more atmospheric, there's really no difference at the end of the night when you've spent most of your rent money on alcohol for your whole group and are too hammered and broke to properly get a cab.

A couple shots in, I notice this not so hottie enter from the rear entrance (I'll let you guess if that's a pub or not), and start eyeing me from behind the bar. He wasn't ugly by any means, but he didn't exactly give me the clit tingling sensation of lust. But regardless, if there's a free drink to be had I can make any guy think he's got what it takes.

A few looks from me and a round of domestic beer is delivered with a, "Hi, I'm Matt. What's your name?"

Does anything about me look domestic? Free is free but Honey please, try again.

A slight smirk and a few more looks and twenty minutes later, a bucket of ice with an expensive bottle of champagne was delivered.

Well done Matt.

Booze started flowing freely on Matt's tab, while flirty conversations between my friend and some older gentleman started to take place. The older gentleman who ended up in our booth was old enough to be our grandfather and also was supposedly "straight". What are you doing in a gay bar on a Friday night then Gramps?

Matt's bottle of bubbly hit me pretty quickly, and sooner than later I was making multiple trips to the ladies room. The best part about going to the restroom at a dominantly male gay bar? The ladies room has no line, and it is the cleanest part of the establishment. Major score when you are far too drunk to put down an ass gasket on the seat to keep the germs from getting at you.

As I made my way to the ladies room for the nth time, I could see Matt eyeing me from across the room in that subtle, "I'm going to fuck your brains proper," sort of way. I decided this time when I went to the bathroom, I was going to prep myself with a diaphragm, so I would be ready to go the minute he was. And with the short, Britney Spears inspired school girl skirt I was sporting, I was already halfway there.

I'm not one to be too cautious in most ventures of my life, but when it comes to birth control I tend to overdo it. I take a double dose of birth control every morning, and even wear the patch. Not completely by choice, because my body did need a higher dose of hormones to keep me from popping out crazy carbon copies of myself. On a few rare occasions where I have needed to head to the pharmacy after a long night of oopsies, and uh-ohs to get the morning after pill, my pharmacist had deemed me, 'Little Miss Plan B.'

As I walked out of the bathroom and down the hall to make my way back to my seat, I was stopped by Matt. He insisted we should give my friend and his old fuck some "alone time", while he "showed me his office". My hands started to shake a bit as I realized the six glasses of Dom I had overly indulged in were about to cost me something.

Shit.

The office was quite spacious, consisting of the furniture you would find more so in a lounge or living room, rather than a work space. The only thing that gave away that it was used to do business was the stacks upon stacks of paper work everywhere.

Matt told me to take a seat, as he circled around the couch lightly touching the back of my neck. While I felt nothing for him, not even the slightest tingle in my stomach, or on my clit, I couldn't help but feel the need to put out. Not just for his sake, but for my own. It had been quite a while since I had gotten laid which was one of the only reasons I really decided to come out tonight. And while he wasn't Mr. Right, or someone I would even consider dating, the amount of alcohol flowing through me made him more than Mr. Right Now.

He sat down next to me, stroking my long, jet black hair behind my shoulder. He leaned in for a kiss, half expecting me to lean in back. But when he got rejected, he quickly dived down to the side of my neck, and worked his way down my shirt line.

I felt a bit antsy and had to stand up for a second. I might have had just a little too much to drink, but not enough to completely cloud my judgment. I stood up and casually walked over to his desk, to play it off that I just wanted to be a bit naughty. He followed like a lamb to the slaughterhouse, and got on top of me and kissed me violently.

The desk was filled with papers, and cash drawers full of crisp Franklins. I lay there, effortlessly, taking every condom wrapped crooked inch that he had to offer. It wasn't enough for me, but it would do for now. Honestly, he could have grabbed the nearest roll of quarters or half dollars and fucked me with it and it would have been significantly bigger and more enjoyable. But I guess the fact we did it on a bunch of freshly printed bills can make even the worst sex some of the best.

He quickly finished before I even got close, and I pulled up my panties and shifted down my skirt to go find my granny fucker of a friend and get the hell out of this joint. I made my way downstairs, found my friend and downed another glass of champagne and chugged it.

We both quickly bolted out the door in the pouring down rain and down the street to find a ticket on the window of my car for parking in a taxi loading zone. The fucked up part is that the ticket was written three minutes before I got out there. Somewhat ironic to get fucked on a mountain of cash, and get fucked for it all within the same night. My friends still joke from time to time, "All that cash and you didn't take any?" Seems to me I might have gotten fucked twice that night.

I Don't Whine

When I say I love wine, I don't think people quite comprehend the magnitude of that statement. I love wine quite possibly more than sex. It's really a close finish between the two especially because both are always good, even when bad. It's like oral sex. It can be bad… but still better than no oral pleasure. And the best oral sex will keep your body hollering for more. This is similar to my love for wine. I always want more.

On this particular day, I had been drinking something of the red variety for a little more than eight hours straight. This was mainly due to the fact I was trying to postpone my third date with Jason, which had become quite a re-occurring event over the past two weeks. The first few dates were the mellow, low-key type which led me to be far beyond sexually frustrated from all the hot tension building up between us.

Jason was a hot, white boy type, who tried a little too hard to be thug...for a lack of better words. But not in the cheesy way, it was more as if it came naturally to him and his swagger would just ooze off of him. He was really into hip hop, but strangely had this smooth voice that made my body melt into a puddle of nothing, almost as if I was entirely wet for him. He could say the most random word in the universe, and I would swoon at the thought and say, 'Take me now.'

I could listen to him talk for hours on end, and a few times, I did just sit on the phone while I tidied up around the house and listen to him babble about God knows what. He wasn't really bright enough to converse with me, but for being Twenty-nine, gorgeous, stunning, dreamy, smooth…give me a moment to compose myself here.

He only lived five blocks away from me too. He had some nice loft overlooking the city that I am sure his parents paid for in full. I envied it nonetheless. But after a full day of wine, I was feeling a bit too horny to try to duck out from another date with him.

I showed up at his door at eleven in the evening. He greeted me with a glass of red wine. This kid was fucking dumb, but he really knew me. And being the polite wino I am, I took the glass with pure excitement and the full intention on fucking him well into the AM.

It was quite unfortunate that there was no real conversation between us that night. I love his voice, and I would love to hear it even more in person. I really don't think he comprehended that his voice was such a turn on in itself. If he did I'm pretty sure he would be off banging every sheila in this town.

There really wasn't even any foreplay. I made the move and took that boy straight to bed, where we both belonged. He didn't seem to mind much at the gesture as he pinned my hands behind my head and began to undress me. Button by button the shirt came off, revealing my perky breasts. He took his sweet time working his way down to my skirt, not even wasting the time to take it off. He slid his hand up my thigh and placed his fingers deep inside of me. Yes, sometimes I forgot to wear underwear to these sort of things. No sense in dirtying up a pair only for a couple of hours especially when they would just get in the way.

He kissed my sides, inch by inch, and made his way past my hip bones and down to my vagina. But instead of licking me, or continuing to finger me, he teased me with a little of both and with a swift motion flipped me over and took me from behind. The sex was not the greatest, but the full wall of windows and a city view made me cum all by themselves. It was a sweaty, and long night... like all great sex should be. But it still ended the same way it always does with the man passing out, allowing me enough time to slip out and head on home to wash the slut off me, once again.

I was still far too drunk to drive home, and frankly I've never been a fan of it. It was only five blocks to walk home, and I really should have opted for that based on the disapproving looks my dogs gave me when I came home. That drive became the longest five blocks of my life. Roughly halfway home, my mouth began to water with the taste of hot red wine.

Uh-oh, I thought to myself. I always know where this is about to go. Just as I began to roll down my window, it happened far too suddenly. A continuous stream of vomit flowed up from my innards like the fat kid who ate too much before the rollercoaster of doom. Foamy, red vomit began to flow everywhere--down my chest and all over my clothes, onto the side of interior, and all over the outside of my car.

After I had finished, and realized the mess I had made I dug through my car to find anything that would do for a quick clean up. I found an old sweater in the backseat which I used to clean up of the car. I wiped down everything, including myself, to the best of my drunken ability, and left my shirt and the sweater at the scene of the crime. I finally made it home, and as tough as it was to walk past my building's security covered in bright red vomit, I held my head very high. The walk of shame may have never been more shameful as it was that night, but damn it all... I'm still fabulous.

The Spray Tanned Sex Act

There are very few things that are both an eyesore and a sex act. Wesley…well, Wesley provided me with both. He was another one of my online dating victims. Actually scratch that, I was the fucking victim. I was the victim of another Los Angeles thirty something who is in the entertainment business.

God, like there aren't enough.

I don't really remember the details. I ate, I drank. He babbled about the accounting department drama at Fox and namedropped like he thought I cared. Truthfully, the only thing running through my mind was how incredibly hot I looked when I checked myself in the bathroom mirror. Skin was a perfect shade of bronze and my tits were even more perfect than usual. I would have gone lesbian for myself.

Anyway… blah, blah, blah. A few more drinks.

This guy is so fucking annoying. Oh well, who am I kidding? I needed to get laid and I was just too damn hot not to get fucked. I was going to make my fresh bikini wax worth it.

So we walked across the street to a bar to "shoot pool". Truth is the only thing I wanted to shoot was alcohol or myself. This guy would not shut the fuck up. I don't normally need bad judgment to fuck a hot guy who looks like Rex from *Days of Our Lives*, but with Wesley it was a requirement. Two shitty games of pool later and lord knows how many drinks. I agreed to go home with him.

As we stumbled out of the bar, I was blinded. Not by lust, nor love, but by his bright orange HUMMER. What the fuck?! This guy drove around in what looked like Cheetos-colored fat cells lipo'd from Snooki's ass. And it's new! He bought this willingly? It was at that moment the plans for how we would arrive at his place changed slightly. I agreed to follow him home. I couldn't bare the embarrassment of being seen in that thing.

For the next twenty minutes, I followed that spray tanned eyesore to his apartment. The entire time contemplating a multitude of things; from suicide, to how I'd rather have cum in my eye or my $800 heels than to drive his car, to possibly calling that guy with the veneers that are far less blinding in comparison. I contemplated until it was too late, his guest parking placard was hanging in my car and I was in his apartment slamming Monster energy drink and Skool vodka. God, did this guy ever graduate college? Am I so drunk I blindly walked into the basement of a frat house? Let's just get this over with.

He led me to his bedroom where he slammed me on his bedroom floor because I was not about to fuck on those cheap bed in bag sheets of his. (Tip: Always invest in nice bedding) We fucked like horny teenagers. Exactly like horny teenagers, I should've taken the hint he didn't know how to use a stick by the way he played pool at the bar. God, I need help. And right there, I lay as he snored until I was sober enough to do the five in the morning walk of shame with his parking pass in hand. The best thing to come of this, free parking in that area of L.A., because it really is a bitch.

My Ex.. Fiance?

It's been a week since I graduated college, and it's still pretty mind blowing. When you're in school, there's just this overwhelming sense of, it's never going to end. Think about how you felt the minute you got into 7th grade and multiply that by a thousand. That still doesn't come close to the intensity and infinity of your college career.

But four long years, and one extra semester later, I was finally ready to say goodbye. Say goodbye to this tiny college town, filled with its small town folk, filled with small town talk. Most people want to stick around and enjoy their graduation ceremony, and have a big party following that with all their friends, family and loved ones. But not I. I wanted to get the hell out of there and as quickly as possible. Lucky enough for me, I was able to conveniently fit my life into the smallest U-Haul truck available in the middle of the night. My escape was flawless.

I did, however, say goodbye to a few ones that mattered to me before I made my 15-hour drive with my soon-to-be-husband, George. My lovely fiancé lived in the city of Angels, a beautiful town I had only dreamed of living in at this point. To make it a more special occasion, he proposed to me on my birthday while I was on one of my weekend trips to visit him and handle some business in southern California. It seemed like the stars were aligning just right for me at this time, and George had become my one way ticket out of my home state.

Windows down and the stereo up, we were speeding down the I-5 screaming lyrics to the cheesy Top 40 songs that were coming on. We stopped at random diners, drive thrus and dive bars for our caffeine fix, while taking our time and enjoying each other's company. We had the sunset on our tails, rushing us to complete the trip in one day. We had planned for a straight shot to Los Angeles, but six hours into the drive I just couldn't take it anymore. And I could see it on his face he needed to let off some steam as well.

I made the brisk move to place my hand on his knee. Almost as if I were going to comfort him. I slowly started building up a grip in my hand and making a massaging motion as I worked my way up to his cock. I ran my hand aggressively up and down the fabric seam in the crotch, until I could feel the bulge beneath it grow harder and bigger. I really had lucked out with this one. He had the most beautiful cock I have ever seen in my life. I am pretty sure that if I were to conduct a search, no one would come close to the shape, size, and power like his penis brought to our sex life. What is even better is that the sex life is only the tip of our relationship; no pun intended. We have such a strong bond mentally and physically, which I'm pretty sure is why we have been together for so long.

I teased him for a little while longer until he couldn't take much more of it. He always gets a twitch in his leg when it becomes too much for him, which is a great sign to know when to take it to the next level. I slowly unzipped his pants and made my hand find it's way through his boxers and onto his skin. I was already so turned on at this point that there was no point on beating around the bush. Again, no pun intended.

I adjusted my seat belt properly and bent over to wrap my luscious lips around his penis. By this point I can feel that my lace panties are just sopping wet. I used my tongue to tickle the underside of his shaft, and bob up and down a couple times before he takes his right hand off the steering wheel and slides his hand up my thigh and straight past my dress. Now, I know I've said previously that I'm totally a jeans and tank type of girl, but I make one exception for putting together a cute dress, and that is road trips. When you're in public and on the road, wearing unnecessary amounts of clothes makes getting freaky on the go just that much harder. A dress, or even a skirt, gives your partner easy access while also allowing you to tease them a bit with a leg or two out the window.

His hand made its way to my vagina, which was radiating with heat. He slid the bottom of my undies over just enough to shift his two fingers inside me. My walls tightened around my vagina as I was almost immediately at climax. I was moaning, screaming, and gripping the side of the door as a dirty trucker drove by our left and saw it all. He gave us the thumbs up sign as he blared his trucker horn numerous times. I was pretty sure we just made his day. I'm not one for the whole public display of affection, but sometimes there is nothing hotter than a little exhibitionism.

I couldn't take it anymore and I screamed for him to slide his seat back a bit. Baffled by my request, yet cooperative, I leapt on top of him and slid his cock inside of me. It was a tight fit, but totally doable. I straddled him and let my ready to orgasm vagina cum all over him. I cum not once, not twice, but three times within the next 20 miles of the drive. He was truly something else when it came to the sex. We didn't even care at this point about anyone noticing us. To him it became a game to see how many times he could get me off before we reached the next rest stop.

He was about ready to cum and made his way to the shoulder of the road to pull over. His little moan in my ear letting me know he was about to cum was more than enough to make me cum again as I hopped off him. He opened his door and came all over on the side of the highway as passerby's honked and cheered. As he turned back to sit comfortably in the driver's seat, I put my lips back around his cock to make sure he was all cleaned up down there. Plus, I loved the taste of him. It's a glorious, and quite delicious thing that I had quickly become addicted to.

We readjusted our clothing and he started the car up to get us going back on schedule. My dripping panties were too much to handle at this moment so I used what was dry on them to wipe off a bit down there and casually toss them out the window as we took off into the final rays of sun set on this day. We stopped at a gas station a decent distance from there and refueled both the car, and our snack bag. Needless to say, we eventually made our way to Los Angeles that night. It just took us a few more hours than expected.

A Week in the Life of Lexa

Veneers, Prince Albert and a midget. How do I even explain how those three things fit together?

I guess it all started with on my first date with a man we shall call, Larry, for certain purposes. A salt and pepper slightly Jewfroed producer of a well-known entertainment news show. We met at a hotel bar in Hollywood. Truthfully, the only thing I found out about "Larry" while sitting across from him was that he had a small dog which is always a good thing, because, you can't trust men who don't like dogs. Even though sometimes the ownership of a small breed means the man is a closeted gay. Larry quickly disproved this theory with a make out session by the valet stand. (Yes, people I'm that classy and I gave him a second date.)

The second date was a party the next night at his house in The Valley. God, I hate The Valley, but I made the trip over Laurel Canyon regardless because very rarely do I pass up the chance for free alcohol.

His neighborhood was nice and quiet with plenty of street parking despite even the various cars of his guests to the party. As he welcomed me into his house, my eye was immediately caught by the most beautiful set of veneered teeth I have ever seen. Just beautiful, and I knew my arrival caught the attention of the very cute boy with them because even in the dim track lighting of Larry's Valley home, the light reflecting off those veneers nearly blinded me as he looked at me. Alas, it only took a second of my best flirty smile before Larry whisked me off for a tour of his three bedroom with a full wet bar... and hot tub, because you know it's The Valley.

So, after an hour or so of polite conversation with complete strangers, taken with plenty of alcohol as any socialite would recommend, I stepped away to collect my thoughts and pop a xanax so that I was able to continue delighting people with my bright personality. As I popped my pill like a Pez and washed it down with an entire glass of champagne, and I overheard the last bit of a conversation that almost made me spit it back up.

It was Sean, a very Bohemian-vibed type of guy talking about how his dick still hurt from being pierced. Now, I'm into this. High School was where many of my firsts took place but a pierced cock is like seeing a unicorn... almost. After realizing that his conversation was overheard by what he thought was a set of delicate ears, he quickly apologized. This was very gentlemanly of a guy who was clothed like a ninety-nine cent store discount bin. His apology though quickly turned into a poor attempt at flirting which I just went with because I was already too drunk to care. Then suddenly we were back on the subject of his member and he asked, "Would you like to see it?" And I simply said "Yes", because what girl doesn't want to see a unicorn, or a pierced dick.

We snuck into one of Larry's five bathrooms, drinks in hand and locked the door behind us. Sean then dropped his pants to his ankles like a three year old at a urinal and pulled out his semi-hard, overly-manscaped, pierced... clit? All I could say was, "Wow" and I'm still not sure if I was commenting on his lack of size or the piercing itself. But I know the bar through the head of it had more length and girth.

After some awkward conversation and the eventual quick exchange of numbers (because I felt bad for him and was too drunk to be a bitch) before I could escape the bathroom and go laugh to myself, I texted the events to my roommate. As I was trying to find another quiet place to steal a moment on my Blackberry, I ran into to the boy with the veneers. He smiled; I went blind. He introduced himself as Eric and we started talking. I learned a few things about him very quickly. One, when he closed his mouth so you could see, he had a perfect body. Two, his accent was Midwestern, which is the type of boy I seem to attract all day long and never really go for because they're too nice. (God, I need even more therapy) Three, the strobing effect when he talked could cause seizures. Then he asked me out. This kid moved fast. I bargained him to taking my number and made my escape back to the center of the party and my date.

The party was shit, much like everything about The Valley, it died around eleven thirty. Larry's offer of an expensive bottle of wine made a convincing case on why I should stay for what he called the after party. Which was just him and I sitting on the couch talking, occasionally being joined by his dog, who was in search of some form of attention. He talked and one bottle of nice wine led to another and another before leading to the clichéd ending of us naked in the hot tub.

I must admit, after being let down by lack of size of my unicorn earlier that night, seeing Larry's salt and pepper pubic hair surrounding what I can only describe as, a Verne Troyer-sized penis, was refreshing. Even though all I could think to myself is how in the hell was I going to cram a midget in my vagina if we ever got that far. Lord, help me. Luckily though, this was not the night I was to experience child birth in reverse.

…………..

Sunday, my day of rest, or it should be. However, Eric must eat sugar for breakfast. I woke up to my phone exploding like a suicide bomber with nine lives. God, it was too early and I had drunk too much.

Text 1: "Good Morning?"

Text 2: "Your smile is so beautiful."

Text 3: "Do you wanna hang out tomorrow night?"

Text 4: "I can come over and bring you dinner and wine and we can watch a movie."

I need to change my number. Fuck, I can't really deal with Sprint this early or this hung- shit I'm still drunk. Whatever, it's a free meal.

……………..

Later that night, and if possible, still drunk from Larry's party and after party, I made my appearance in Santa Monica, looking like a hot mess.

May I stress the "hot" part?

We met at some wine bar off Main Street where he was apparently a regular. Showing he had class and setting him apart from my normal realm of douche bags. He ordered us some amazing Pinot Noir that paired perfectly with the food. Truthfully, when a man steps up and orders for a woman, it's a make or break moment. Luckily, for Eric it made him and further set him apart. We ate, we chatted and ended the night with a solid kiss before I got back in my car and started my drive back to Hollywood. I would've loved to corrupt that shy innocence of his, sadly though he ended our date at 9:45 like he was a sixteen year old with a curfew. But it was refreshing to know I was going to get a full night's sleep before work tomorrow.

Ring

I swear to God Eric, I left you like ten minutes ago... Oh my God, the disappointing unicorn wants to have a drink. Free booze, my one motivating factor for being nice.

I met Sean at a bar in Hollywood were we shared nothing any deeper than our alcoholism. He paid the tab when I thought we were about to head our separate ways so I could get some sleep before going to my nine-to-five hell, but he asked me for a ride home. Why not continue with the kindness? After all he's basically a eunuch. I kindly drove him to his apartment and he invited me in. Here's where I question my decision making. He invited me in... I accepted. He offered me a beer... I accepted. And somehow I ended up letting the pierced human Ken doll dry hump me. I can't really explain it. It just happened on the hideaway bed in his studio apartment. I don't know if you can even call it sex. There was no way he penetrated me. Thank God he fell asleep right after.

……………..

It's sad being at work and realizing the man with the most beautiful teeth, fake or not, is clingy and insane. His texts made it sound like I was trying to hide a defective vibrator in my desk. Finally, I took the time on my lunch break to respond simply, "I had a great time. I will let you know when we can hang out." Truthfully, I never read all of his 207 text messages, and I contemplated not ever seeing or speaking to him again. But the way those teeth out shined the sun… okay maybe I will see him again.

………………..

Once again, here I am driving over this fucking canyon. Whatever, he's taking me to dinner at Katsuya, so it's worth the traveling. I park, go in for one vodka drink. We leave for dinner. It's amazing. But yet again it's Katsuya, should I expect less than amazing?

After dinner and wine it's back to The Valley. I am sitting in the same spot on his couch as last week. Do I like Larry? Not really sure. Do I like him enough to sleep with him? Well, yeah, of course.

The foreplay began on the couch as his dog watched from the floor by the fireplace. Clothes fly off, I straddled him on the couch as he planted kisses all over my naked body. We then moved it to his bedroom and all I could think to myself is "Where's the anesthesiologist with the epidural?"

I took it though. I was forced to break two of my rules: Never stay the night and never stay the night in The Valley. But I really couldn't move afterwards so, thank god for Seinfeld reruns.

. . . .

God damn--my vagina hurts. Pregnant bitches get to at least spend a week in the hospital after that kind of vaginal trauma. Larry--if there's ever a next time--Larry he's going to need to find a more expensive place to take me to dinner to make this worth it.

Fuck… I promised to meet veneer boy today. Ugh.

. . . .

Being the Midwestern gentleman that he was, he let me park in his parking garage and met me downstairs. Sigh… he was gorgeous, even though he was clingy. He also lived alone in a beach front apartment that everyone should be jealous of.

When I walked into his apartment the first words out my mouth were, "I want to live here." I felt blessed by God that when I turned around to face him after saying that, he wasn't down on one knee with a ring. His place was the second most beautiful thing I've ever seen. The first being what I see every morning when I look into the mirror.

I sat down on his couch and he greeted me with a glass of amazing red wine. Then every girl's dream happens... he brings out four huge bags of hair, skin, and beauty products for me to take home with me. God, at that moment I loved this kid. I should've have said it. I bet the next gift would've been Harry Winston.

We continued to drink wine and watched some dumbass movie called "The Hangover", obviously written by idiots who've never been drunk a day before in their life. He laughed; I didn't. We talked afterwards and it was really an amazing date.

Then he politely asked me to spend the night. To which I had to ask myself, "Can my vagina take this?"

I decided it was going to.

This kid's bedroom is clean and pretty--what the fuck? I lay down in his bed and left my underwear on so I didn't seem like a true slut. We started making out, hands all over each other's bodies.

His body was hot--eight pack, great tight ass. He was like a teenage girl's (or in my case a mid-twenties girl's) wet dream. He clearly knew how to please a woman with his mouth based on how many orgasms I had. Even his cock was beautiful. So I did it. I slept over, and didn't leave until like nine the next morning. We had sex three times throughout.

And I left with my bag of beauty products and the knowledge that I just fucked the most beautiful man with veneers one night after having a midget crammed into my uterus.

I'm a Pussy for Jager

I like to consider myself as straight as they come, but even pasta, which is straight, gets a little questionable when it gets hot! So when I had the opportunity to have sex with a chick, well, it just happens.

Let me just tell you from plenty of experience, the walk of shame after a night with a woman is remarkably similar except that I felt far more sexually satisfied with far less slut. As I walked my way to the car that morning I thought, "God, I need a coffee."

But there was no hangover, and I felt a bit far too wobbly for it being 5am. Fuck, I'm still drunk. Fuck it, I need some Taco Bell.

I had a dry, cotton mouth that morning except for the terrible taste that lingered between the moist spots of my mouth. It was a God awful combination of Jager and Pussy. And it was the worst. The Jager, not the pussy.

Saturday mornings shouldn't be a recuperating day as this is the time to keep the party going and get ready for a night to do it all again. Much so like a Katy Perry song.

Racking my brain, I was able to backtrack through foggy memories and text messages to learn what exactly happened. I went out with my gays on Friday night, and we did our normal bar hopping through West Hollywood extravaganza. This usually ended up double fisting adult beverages at some shitty dance club. It's one of those clubs that you have to be drunk to enjoy, and if you aren't then you are going to be bored out of your mind. Yeah, it's pretty much like every club out there. And that's where I met Lydia.

Lydia was this beautiful, stylish chick. Total Hollywood sweetheart, if you catch my drift. Great eye candy, but it really killed my buzz anytime she attempted to talk. I had seen her out a couple of times before but never really talked to her since she was on the outer most part of my circle of friends.

We ended up needing a cigarette at the same time and so we found ourselves on the outside smoking patio at the same time. And this brought us into our first real conversation. And by conversation I mean her unloading on me about her recent break up with her boyfriend who she thought was the one. You know young love drama. I never really was one to fall for that type of cliché, but I know what it's like to be hurting even if I can't directly relate it to love.

She tried to justify that maybe it was a good thing, because they needed a break. But I was thinking, no. If you need a break, you shouldn't really be together. It still baffles me that in a world full of billions of people, individuals try to hold on for far too long when nothing is there that is worthwhile. But I didn't want to tell her to shut up. I was just being polite for the rules of "Girl Talk." I went above and beyond the call of duty though with that, and the conversation finally got into a topic that was juicy enough for me to pay attention.

"As of lately, I've been questioning my sexuality quite often."

Before I get into this, I want to take time to explain a few things. First, all women have come to the conclusion at one point or another that they should pitch for the other team for a bit. It's almost like a rite of passage now. If you haven't made out or felt up another girl by the time you hit high school, it's almost like you're the freak now. Secondly, if you haven't noticed from what you've read so far, when I'm out and about on the town I only drink beer and champagne. Sometimes when I'm in the right mood, I'll dabble into a little bit of vodka, but shots are a big, "Hell no."

But yet, last night was a special night. She offered to buy some Jager shots in honor of our new found pussy power, and the girl talk started and the pressure mounted from our mutual gays to *join their team.* Of course, the giggles to that only encouraged another shot of Jager, followed by another and we all know where this was headed with the velocity and toxicity that goes hand in hand with Jager.

This is why I was sitting in my car, in a dress that's far too short with no panties on at a Taco Bell drive-thru.

This is where the night started to get blurry though. I lived close to the club we were at. And my roommate at the time, Tim, was a go-go dancer there. So I would frequent the club just to cheer him on from time to time. I could have easily saved myself the lesbian walk of shame and took her home, but that's not my style. Instead, I was in the backseat of a car driving thirty-five minutes to West Los Angeles just to fool around with Lydia. When we got to her place, I distinctly recall falling ass first into the bushes outside the car, only to fall face first into her arms when she helped me up. What a lame move even in my drunken stupor. I remember a lot more champagne and random bong hits when we finally got to her house, and I remember briefly that she disappeared. From there all I know is I continued to rip from the bong and got more wasted till my urge to fall asleep was becoming a fighting urge not to black out.

I looked around the apartment for Lydia, and ended up finding her in the kitchen drinking some water. She told me she was going to lie down and I was far too fucked up to say anything but follow her back like a lost puppy dog. I couldn't even lie down on her bed. Instead, it became a quick fall into the bed and becoming incapable of moving. It almost felt like I had been drugged, but then I had to remind myself of how much I actually drank, and that this was going pretty easy on my body.

The minute I lay down she was all over me. Violently kissing me and ripping my favorite shirt off and into shreds before hitting the floor. What a violent and wild one this Lydia was. Completely not what I expected, I wanted to yell rape, but I was too wasted, so instead I thought, fuck it, and went along with it. I mean why not. I know this wasn't her first time at the pink taco bar. And she was far too good at the way she massaged my breasts and caressed my curves for me to even consider telling her the cliché statement, "No means no."

She started to pull off my dress, and I was so wet I was afraid I might have accidentally pissed myself somewhere between falling in the bush and landing in her bed. I couldn't tell if it was just beginner's luck with her, or if she had a copy of *Shelling the Clam for Dummies* stashed in her cunt. Either way, the orgasm was better than most of the men I had ever been with. Between the hair pulling and spanking, some guys could really learn a lesson from this chick.

Around the time of the orgasm was around the time I had blacked out, or passed out. Not sure which happened first, but it was definitely something I wish I could be feeling right now. My head throbbed in pain as the hangover started to finally kick in. Talk spread quickly through our friends to the point where it's still this ongoing joke between many of us. Girls will do silly things, like each other in this case. Oh well, let's just hope I don't have another sex tape lurking the depths of the internet again from this time around.

Love, Like or Whatever

I can count on one hand how many times I've met someone and thought to myself, "Can we just fast forward 10 years and be together then?" This is the case with Greg. By now I'm sure you understand that I rarely catch feelings for anyone. I keep my heart chained up and guarded better than anyone. Greg is handsome, funny, caring and even comes equipped with an adorable midwestern accent. Little did I know that I would have such an intense connection with a silly match.com date.

Our first date was close to perfection especially for a first date. We had exchanged a few basic emails and flirty text messages before agreeing to meet in person. I live downtown and he lives by the beach in Santa Monica. We decided to meet in the middle at this small wine bar. At this point, I know he read my entire profile and didn't just jerk off to my profile photo. He read about my love for wine. One point for him. I remember seeing him for the first time and thinking he's the cutest damn thing I've ever seen. He's the opposite of what I usually date. He has a killer smile. We hit it off immediately over similar tastes in fine wine, our addiction to food (did I mention he cooks? I love a man who cooks) and just overall chemistry that even I myself cannot put into words onto paper. After we sampled a variety of red wines from all over the world, we decided to continue our date over a meal next door on the patio. While sitting across the table talking to Greg, I found myself falling for his innocent charm between my overtly sarcastic and flirty comments. It's a strange feeling when I don't lose immediate interest in someone. The conversation flowed through the entire dinner. We laughed, he offered to walk me to my car, but I only let him walk me to the stoplight (just in case he was a sexy serial killer.. hello.. remember Ted Bundy?) But even if he was a serial killer I let him kiss me--in front of pedestrians, in front of everyone who was driving by that exact intersection. Who the fuck am I? I hate public displays of affection. And this was the beginning of my online date that even to this day, has no expiration date.

On my second date with Greg, he met me downtown at an Asian restaurant near my place. Once again, the booze was filling the third chair at our table. Ladies, when you want something just fucking go for it. That's what I did. I wanted to get naked with this midwest boy and dirty up his sheets. And that is exactly what I did. I followed him to his beach apartment so that I could of course have my car as my getaway car. We got to his place and to be quite honest, it's a huge blur of sweaty nakedness. The parts I do remember though, are vivid. I remember him making me moan and cum with his tongue. I remember every inch of his body, and I remember making intense eye contact during our fuck session.

After these two dates, Greg and I continued to text, make plans to hang out more often, etc. but we just never made it work. I take a lot of the responsibility for this one. I was flighty, young, wanted to be single, but in the back of my head and deep in my dark, dark soul, I always thought we should be together. At one point, I was in a serious relationship. At another point, he was in a serious relationship. The timing was always, and continues to be to this very day, just off. We would drunk dial each other at 3 AM asking each other "Why the fuck aren't we together?" and we just never made it happen.

Fast forward five years: Here we are. Five years older and full of experience that we didn't have when we first met at that wine bar. We are both single, living in different time zones and always making plans to visit and spend quality time together. The common denominator between Greg and I can be described in one word: FEAR. We both have this disgusting fear of commitment, and I admittedly have a fear of falling in love with him. So here we are two successful and attractive individuals who share a deep connection and a raw and never ending love for one another and we just refuse to make it work.

We've hooked up over the years here and there and everywhere--randomly on his layovers at LAX, dinner, drinks, the usual. We always manage to pick up where we left off. Weeks, months and even years can pass with little or no communication between us, and we still have some fucked up magnetic energy that seems to have a rechargeable battery built right into it. We balance each other out in ways that make no sense to the rest of the world. I'm a wild, bold and crazy woman who will make a man's life a living hell. He is the opposite. He's a gentleman who for some reason is attracted to my inner crazy and fucked up emotional disconnect.

Currently, our relationship remains as great friends. Even though we care about one another beyond the definition of a friendship. I'm strangely vulnerable with him (which

I hate), and he drives me crazy and can annoy the shit out of me. That's more than lust right?

I guess timing is everything and even I'm capable of falling in "like" or "love" or whatever.

5 Years in 3 Dates and This is Taking it Slow

Oh, happy hour on the rooftop bar of The Standard Hotel downtown...beautiful view, shitty plastic champagne flutes, LA's version of the bridge and tunnel crowd and some of my best, sexcapades.

I was meeting my good friend from work for drinks to catch up on office gossip over a couple of drinks. I noticed this tall, handsome brunette guy with wavy hair, and I toldl my friend "Oh my God, he is so hot. I need to talk to him." I rarely meet men at "bars" or "clubs", but damn. My friend, being the amazing wingman that he is, approached Mr. Tall Brunette and asked him for a cigarette, despite not having a nicotine addiction although he enjoys a good oral fixation.

Of course, Mr. Tall Brunette was happy to donate one of his mini phallic objects to my friend. And after laying eyes on me, he then sat down across from us for some small talk. I mean who wouldn't? Have you seen me?

His name was Brett. He lives in Los Angeles. We exchanged numbers and 20 minutes after his departure from the Standard Hotel, he texted me.

We had made plans to meet at a local bar the next evening for drinks. I showed up to the bar and there he was again, outside smoking his fancy cigarettes. I drank a few beers, met a few of his buddies and then quickly found out that he has a motorcycle. I swoon for men with motorcycles. (They're like giant vibrators.)

I somehow end up agreeing to going riding in the Santa Monica mountains the VERY NEXT DAY. Take note-this will make seeing Brett 3 days in a row. I can barely tolerate myself for 3 days in a row, let alone a man, even multiple men in that time span. Shoot me. But I can't pass a day of riding up, so I go.

It's a Sunday, void a walk of shame. Rare, but pleasant. I meet him at his beautiful home off of Mullholland Drive. He is just as gorgeous on an early Sunday morning as he was the previous two nights. His home is a gorgeous open space and he lives alone. Okay, this could be good I told myself. He gives me a brief tour, fits a helmet on my head as I gage how I'd fit him in me, and we are ready to hit the open road.

I am a pro at being a passenger on the back of a bike, however, I was a little nervous and untrusting in the beginning of the ride. But shortly after we reached Sunset Blvd and took it all the way to the PCH, I was feeling right at home. And I didn't even mind spending time with him. We weaved all around the coast and made several stops along the way to eat, catch a beer and the view. We went past Pepperdine all the way to Zuma Beach and then back through the mountains. By the time we made it back to his house my ass hurt worse than from any sexual ass play I had ever experienced. I had made previous plans with my friend Ian and some other friends to play bar trivia. Brett asked to tag along and for some reason I agreed. Fuck, I wasn't thinking at all. Now he was going to meet my REAL friends?

I showered at his house. I found it strange when he didn't try to join me. He just left me a towel on the counter… he even shut the door. "Did I actually meet a gentleman?"

We met my friends at trivia along with two of his friends he took the "liberty" of inviting as well. Everything was going great until he fucking went bi-polar. I don't have patience or time for escaped mental patients. Fuck him. (Not literally)

He ended up talking to my buddy Ian outside of the bar for a good 30 minutes as I continued to kick ass at trivia, because I'm a genius, and pounded pitchers of beer. The trivia game ends (we came in 2nd place) and I now had to drive this asshole all the way back up Mulholland, drunk. Ugh.

We argued the whole way in the car, he threatened to get out and walk home like a psycho douche. It's like we've been together for five years. I have trouble doing five months, so this was disgusting. We reached his house, and I was way too drunk to drive all the way back home, so he offered his couch. I said, "Fuck you and your couch, I will come in for a glass of water and leave in an hour".

To top this sundae of mental disorders. for the past three days I had asked Brett what he did for a living, but he never answered me. I'm a real estate savant, and his home was worth at least 2.5 million dollars. So, at some point he had to have an occupation. He got very defensive every time I would ask him, which was a red flag. He tried to tell me some fake ass story about how he "inherited" money, then changed it and said he received a large "settlement" from his previous employer. Asshole.

We talked in his bedroom for an hour while I tried to sober up and drive home. He ended up apologizing and trying to get all deep about his childhood on me. Kill me now. Deep inside me is all I want from a guy. Deep emotions are overrated.

He ended up kissing me, I ended up naked under his white sheets with his head between my legs. The white sheets were the only thing good about it. I assumed at this point we are going to "go all the way" but no, someone wanted to "take things slow"? His face remained between my legs until 3 AM. When he came up for air he whispered the creepiest shit like "Lexa, you have no idea how amazing your pussy is."

Uh… yes I fucking do.

Forgetting psychos like Brett is why I drink. He added at least five years to my alcoholism.

First Class Whore

For a while I did a lot of traveling whether it was for odd jobs or for pure, unadulterated pleasure..Traveling had become an overly guilty pleasure of mine. But I wasn't really the type that was ready to go road tripping with friends across the country listening to shitty top 40 music on the open highway. I preferred to get a plane ticket and travel alone--take a plane trip to some place far away from my current existence, and meet new, like-minded individuals.

I didn't just enjoy a simple plane trip though. I really liked to get ahead of myself and splurge with the extra cash for that round trip, first-class ticket. The best part of flying first class is the free booze, and I find it my personal duty to drink the price difference of the ticket between it and coach. Any other seat on the plane, I would be getting a few beverages compliments of some lonely business man who wants to join the mile-high club while getting ready to be a guest on the next episode of Jerry Springer. Well, the best way to avoid those creepers altogether is just pay the extra.

Before the recent TSA security and safety policies for plane rides, I actually used to sneak an empty water bottle on the plane and dump drink after drink into it right before they did their version of "last call." This would really help out with the trip from the airport to the hotel, or a friend's house in every city, state and country I would visit.

However, this flight was a bit different. It was two weeks before Christmas, and I was broke. I mean, with my drinking, being broke was always bound to happen. But I was on the plane, drinking the same old free booze, but this time it had a purpose. The alcohol wasn't to calm my nerves, or loosen me up for a crazy getaway. This time, I was drinking and taking it all in as fast as I could to forget--forget everything that had happened the past six days. I wanted to forget about myself, and to forget all about him. It was the most life-changing experience in the most devastating way. And it was my first and last time as a hooker.

I started going through this phase, almost kind of being a gold digger, but genuinely looking for a more well-off soul mate. I like money, and I like to spend it, roll around in it and smell it. But mostly I like to spend it. And while I had been working my damn ass off to barely get by, it wasn't emotionally satisfying to me to sit around and do so much with my life, but so little for it. So I started taking up the option that was so playfully given to me by a friend about looking for a sugar daddy. I wasn't sure exactly where to start, but a few Google searches turned up more than enough information over the course of a few minutes.

A few sites later and I found myself the perfect place to score a rich man who was desperate enough to let me be his arm candy. That really shouldn't be too hard since I am perfect for that. Long legs, perfectly tanned skin, beautiful long dark hair, and the perfect petite body. But I digress.

I met a man by the name of Chris. He was a bit on the older side, but that was something I was willing to overlook. Judging some of his photos, he was almost a George Clooney-esque sort of character. It started off as a few messages through the site, which lead to emails. I always like to start with the email process first because it's easier to block an email address, or flag it as spam, than it is to change a number. After enough screening I gave him my number with a little "winky" and told him to text me some time. And after a countless number of texts, we progressed to actual phone calls.

If you know me, you would realize that this is a huge commitment. It's not really a fear of the phone like most individuals suffer from. I just genuinely hate lifting anything to my mouth that isn't food or champagne. And maybe the occasional blow job. It's unfortunate that despite my phone's delicious name as a Blackberry, it hardly ever gets the honor of my oral fixation.

After feeling comfortable enough with my future "Jon" we eventually got onto the topic of him planning a special trip for me to Los Angeles. It really was the least he could do. I rarely have entitlement issues, but when it comes down to me putting out so much of myself to one individual, I really do expect a lot in return. It doesn't matter if it's physically with materialistic possessions, or if it's with emotional connections. Just give me something to feel and hold on to.

He planned the trip and emailed me the itinerary. He was far more into the whole idea of this than I was. Frankly, I was just excited to leave my college town and get into Los Angeles for a bit. I had so many plans to move here in the next few years that I loved traveling there every chance I got.

I made my way to the airport, and onto the plane. Same shit, different day. Security pat downs, lines, shitty and overpriced food. Sometimes I wonder if airports are secretly owned by Disneyland, or some other amusement park. I waited probably an hour before my plane was ready to board. And we sat on the runway another 45 minutes due to a flight delay. But they started serving some beverages while we were stuck, so I had no complaints. And thank God that Chris wanted the best for me with this first-class upgrade on my ticket.

When I landed, he was waiting there at the luggage carousel for me with a dozen roses and a sign with my name on it. Typical, but a great first impression. I got in his brand new Jaguar, my tan legs soaking up the California sun with the windows down. It felt good to be in a city that I have always felt at home in. But unfortunately, it wouldn't be so homely this time around.

He took me to some cute and cozy cafe off Melrose for dinner. After much conversing I found out he was B-O-R-I-N-G! This kind of came as quite the surprise after all the emails, texts and even calls we had up to this point. I couldn't tell if he was just nervous or that personality he had showed me was just another facade, like the rest. Clearly it had to be the latter seeing as he had to pay for a woman to show any interest in him.

Two bottles of wine later and I really had zero dirt on him. The only thing that really came out was the fact he had two daughters who were each three years younger than me. Pretty gross dating someone who could be your dad, but I've heard far worse for less cash. Besides, he tried so hard to be sweet that I felt like a royal cunt pushing the boundaries on that specific topic.

After I had a great buzz going on, we headed to the Beverly Hilton. Some of my best work had been done there. From writing to nights I would never forget. Unfortunately, this was a night that I wish I could forget.

Chris didn't invite me up to the hotel. In fact, he really didn't even try to kiss me. I sat in the lobby and waited. That's a pretty huge insult to swallow for someone who prides herself in being sexually empowered. And I am not one to swallow.

This began my brief career as an escort. Chris had told me that in order to see me again he offered to fly me home with the only circumstance that I spend two days with him. The rest could be with any of my friends, or even family. I gasped at the chance, knowing that I wouldn't have enough to escape home for the holidays. But being the smart college educated woman that I am, I knew that it meant I was going to have to put out. So I would get a round trip, first class plane ticket for sex. To be honest, I've put out for less.

I flew from sunny Los Angeles to the cold, snow ridden land of Oregon. And before we even landed it was awkward with my "Jon" from the start. I just had to keep cracking the frozen layer off my face in order to remind myself to keep smiling. Keep smiling like any other slutty girl.

But I wasn't just another slutty girl, and it was really only for these two days that I just had to pretend I was. As I stepped off the plan and onto the bridge creating unity between plane and airport, I had to really convince myself that what I was doing here was right. As the coldness of Oregon bit my skin, it was really easy to remind myself why I had left.

The original two days I had planned to stay with him quickly turned into six due to the fact I got snowed in at the old man's mini-mansion in the countryside. Somehow, I wouldn't have doubted if he actually had this planned. My sarcasm screamed, "Fun". At least he had a wine cellar that was as big as an entire downtown apartment. So I wouldn't have to suffer this karmic injustice sober.

Six days spent in a beautiful house, with gorgeous marble statues, fireplaces always blazing, and breathtaking views, and the pathetic excuse of a man only fucked me three times. The first was completely unbearable. He made me do him sober. The whole time he rammed his penis into me was completely off beat accompanied with a normal in and out motion. Clearly this man has no musical bone in his body. Otherwise keeping at least to a beat with his boring in and out motion wouldn't be nearly as bad.

Shortly after banging it out, he forced me into wrapping Christmas presents for his daughters. Now, I normally wouldn't object to helping out around a household, but the fact that he was paying me to be his sex slave for the week and then subjecting me to emotional bonding was just too much for me. I didn't have a problem screwing the man, but when it came down to pretending I care about his life is where it became a problem.

The last two times I fucked him, I had time to get plastered beforehand. This helped me not notice how terrible the sex truly was, or the fact that I had such an old and wrinkled cock inside of me. It might be a little fucked up to admit, but I was terrified that he might have a heart attack while doing me. Even moreso, I was afraid his penis would just tear off from the force he was using behind it.

Six long days, and six long nights was all it took to completely ruin the experience of being a high class hooker. And now, as I'm writing this, I am sitting on the plane almost in tears hoping that there are enough mini shots on this plane to help me forget. The life of a working girl isn't easy, and this doesn't mean that I'm completely hanging up my heels by any means. But I am definitely not doing *this,* or Chris again.

Yoga is Not a Turn On

With so many married, gay, freak and geeks that work at my office it was very hard to find a datable man. Well there is one exception.

I worked in a corporate prison cell or as management calls it, a cubicle. Mine is decorated like a fifteen-year-old girl's locker though. Picture pink boas, photos of my biggest crush (myself) and clippings from fashion magazines everywhere. James, the exception, has his prison cell three doors down from mine and he is forced to walk past mine before he can do anything productive at the office.

He's got the whole Hank Moody thing going with his six-foot-three frame which I found hot as fuck at twenty-six. Honestly, even now I found it hot.

It was a year before James and I even spoke. But a sometimes a few flirty glances can express all that needs to be said. But the exchange of sexual fluids would've been nice.

James, even at his worst always looked good. This made it a running joke between all the single and not so single girls that he might be gay. So one day when my clit was in need of a serious rubbing, the challenge was set before me to prove or disprove the water cooler theory of James sexuality. And I took it.

So I turned it on. I did everything we women do to get men to notice us without ever having to say a word. James was smooth though. He played the same game and forced me to say the first words. And he did it in the most unique way with a key lime pie he dropped off at my desk without a word. This, of course, forced me to get up and walk to his turf to say my flirtiest, "Thank you" before exchanging hot emails leading to numbers and going on our first date.

By the way… the pie itself tasted like shit.

Before we get into the fucking, which is what I know you're all looking forward to, here are a few fun facts you need to know about James:

- He loves Burning Man (which is my worst nightmare)

- He loves doing yoga (this comes in handy to know later)

- He's a bit of a womanizer (and a douche bag)

The first date was good. He picked me up in a silver BMW, and every woman will tell you a hot car is a quick way to moisten her panties. You could be Channing fucking Tatum, but if you drive a piece shit, you are not getting between a woman's thighs. Anyway, dinner on the beach followed by some bar hopping, it went well honestly despite the fact that our only similarities revolved around alcohol, the random line of cocaine and both of us being hot as hell. But that's enough right?

He dropped me off and then asked to "come in and cuddle." Uh, ew. We found a flaw in James. Number one, I don't fuck in my own bed ever! I mean I bring the vagina to the party, you can't expect me to clean up after it too. Number two, "cuddle"? What does he think I am a thirteen-year-old virgin? Hell, even then I didn't "cuddle".

After two more dates and zero "cuddle time" I finally fucked him, at his place. And he was as perfect naked as he was with clothes on. I mean perfect.

Okay, remember that yoga part earlier? This is where it becomes relevant. We did all of the foreplay you can imagine. The usual shit. We then started actually fucking, me on the bottom and him on top. Then he got into this whole "yoga" mode, where he just stayed inside of me and didn't move, practicing his breathing. At this point, I was going along with it even though I've never done yoga in my life. I mean the sex was hot but with the whole stopping to practice deep breathing…it made it impossible to cum. I mean if we were in doggie, I would have been on my Blackberry replying to emails or writing this.

Hotness and a convenient lay go a long way though. I continued to abuse him as a fuck buddy for over a year. But as always, never in my bed and I was always gone by 5 AM.

And no, I never took up yoga.

The Chef

I am a self proclaimed reality television whore, trapped somewhere in between the romanticism and desperateness of women on The Bachelor to every hour-long reality show that Bravo has ever made. Reality television has quickly become an addiction for me, making my addiction with food look miniscule in comparison. But at least my addiction with food isn't like the norm. I pretty much have developed an addiction to just trying new foods. I try new foods from different cultures, go to new restaurants, it's really something I have become so good with that I should have considered a career change, but I prefer to keep my love of food as an indulgence.

But let's be honest, I've been on so many different dates in this city that it's actually quite shocking why I'm not a top food critic for the LA Times. Los Angeles is quite the bottomless pit when it comes to dining out, even takeout and delivery!

Since I have lived here, I have gotten heavily into this popular competitive cooking show. Saying I am heavily into it is quite the understatement, seeing as it combines both my food and reality tv show addiction into one. The first episode I watched during this season, I came across the hottest chef, who just so happens to live and work in Los Angeles. He caught my eye so much I would watch each episode religiously when it aired, as opposed to getting to it later on my DVR. I would tweet him once and a while on Twitter wishing him luck, and blatantly flirting, and every now and then he would reply and return the favor with a few flirty comments back. This had started to go back and forth for the next month, which I was more than okay with.

The chef was a little shy, but definitely more than curious about me. I'd send him sexy photos of me from time to time and he'd reply with the norm, "You're so hot," or "'Oh the things I'd do to that body of yours." Typical horny-guy responses. But there was more than enough juice there to know that he wanted to spread me all over his grill.

Being the aggressive one that I am, I decided it was time to make the next move. I offered to meet up with him but he never took the bait and instead, would mostly ignore it like he never saw it. His lack of interest in meeting just made me more inclined to pursue him. It had been a few months of me asking and asking, and I was just about to give up because I am totally not the desperate type when my phone chimed with an incoming email. I unlocked my phone and opened up the email to find one from him. It was roughly 11 PM and I had a few glasses of wine in me by this point. He asked if I wanted to come over to his house for a drink. But that was it. There was nothing else in there. Just a simple one sentence email. He had clearly been drinking as well, which was a good thing.

I quickly hopped up out of bed and touched up my make up from earlier in the day. It didn't take more than five minutes to get from my sexy lingerie bedtime get up to my hottie and naughty casual look. I had been waiting for over a month at this point to actually hang out with the guy in the flesh and it was finally happening! We had never even had a phone call or video chat up to this point. It was strictly all Twitter and emails! So, this was a very big step for him, and completely random as well.

I showed up at his apartment almost as a nervous wreck. I hadn't had one of those giggly, boy-crazed school girl crushes for years. Even quite possibly almost a decade! But here I was standing at his doorstep shuffling my feet with sweaty palms too scared to touch the doorbell.

I started to analyze my outfit as I waited for him to come to the door. Holy fuck, I went against all my rules and wore flats. What the fuck was I thinking? Flats are the least sexy thing you can wear with any outfit, heels add an easy boost of sexy and make your legs and ass look flexed at all times. But I guess he'll just have to deal with the fact I'm not fully done up seeing as he was the one to ask me to come over at midnight. The shoes will probably just come right off anyway.

Aside from the shoe meltdown, I looked killer. I wore my skinny jeans with zippers up the sides of the ankles, and my deal maker low cut lace tank top and leather jacket combo. He finally came downstairs and greeted me with one of the most comfortable hugs I had come to enjoy in my lifetime and immediately offered me a drink. I drank a Vodka and Sprite because it was all I needed to get my buzz back to where it was.

He then proceeded to ask me if I would like a tour of his place. Ladies, if any guy ever asks if you would like to see their place, they mean would you like to go to the bedroom now or later. Of course I said yes, but as he showed me the bedroom where he had some artwork that he had painted himself that I admired for a few minutes… he has a thing for painting… let's say… body parts of women. So we both made our way back to the couch and stuck up a very pleasant conversation while catching up on some TV. We discussed pretty much everything, which in my opinion is a great start to a guy if I can tell them that much about my twisted little world. What made it even better is he actually got my dry, sarcastic sense of humor and was able to throw back at me some of his own. It was a very comforting feeling having someone capable of reciprocating that side of me, because it is often taken in such a negative context that it sometimes gets disheartening when others can't keep up or think you have gone too far.

I sip glass after glass of Vodka and Sprite for the next two hours. Time flies with such agility when you're buzzed and enjoying the company of another. It was so pleasant I noticed we hadn't even made a physical move at all towards cuddling. It was all just playful banter and flirting with a slice of intellect on the side. It's 2 AM at this point and the late night reruns of Jerry Springer started to play. He took that as his cue to yawn and "sleepily" lay his head down across my lap. Perfect.

I took my arm and rested it on his upper back and began my techniques of being the master seductress that I am. I started by giving him the slightest massage on the back of his neck, easing my way into the base of his skull and working my fingers through his hair. As he moaned with approval, I began my way down his back and towards the front side. He quickly tugged on the bottom of his shirt and I helped him pull it off a bit. His toned and tan body underneath was far from what I expected from him. I kept massaging his back in full this time, and worked him into a position where I was sitting on top of him as he lay face first across the couch. I straddled him, making my hips move with ever massaging motion I made up and down his back. As he got more comfortable and relaxed at the thought of my hands touching him, he turned over to face me. I gently massaged his chest and arms until he pulled me down on top of him and we began the most sensual make out session I have ever participated in. It was pure chemistry, and if someone could measure the heat or temperature of it, I'm sure it would break the thermometer.

There was no romantic or swift motion to pick me up and carry me to the bedroom like most gentlemen. I frankly don't even know how we made it to the bedroom. Everything was a spinning, swirling, twisting, passionate blur.

He pushed me down on the bed and started removing my clothes piece by piece, and even inch by inch. Slowly, but surely they all came off. He started to kiss my body all over but I'm in the mood to take control. I pushed him down on the bed and used one hand to take off his jeans while the other is gripping his hip bone roughly. As the jeans came off, they revealed his already rock hard cock ready for my taking. I scratched my nails along his side as I licked my way down to his penis. My lips began to kiss it softly, while my tongue tickled the bottom side of the shaft. His hand went from gripping my shoulder to pulling my hair so hard I had to come up. He pulled my hair all the way so my head would be directly over his.

He kissed me before he violently pushed me over on the bed and starts making his way down south. There are no words to describe what happened next. While he returned the oral pleasure, I can't help but think that chefs must be the most talented individuals when it comes to sex. I came three times.

The next step naturally would be to fuck. I mean, it's always been that way with every guy I have slept with, but not for him. He wouldn't allow for it at least not on the first "date" or "meeting." As hot as he had gotten me, I respected his wishes. It's funny how him denying sex actually made me crush on him even harder.

The next morning I woke up to a text from him asking if I was tired. Well, no. I'm not tired from driving home like a real whore at 4 in the morning. But, of course, I didn't say that and kept my tongue mildly mannered with a nice reply. We texted every day from this point. I might be a bit of an insomniac, but I still would wait up at night for his late night emails to tell me good night. I started to think that I may be a bit more emotionally committed to this then I had planned. I guess this is what it's like to have feelings.

We both finally had a free spot in our schedule to make another date, and decided to go to dinner at this new restaurant on Pico Blvd. Neither of us had been to it, so it was definitely quite the venture. Our dinner reservation was for 9pm, a bit late for a meal but just early enough to still get the drink specials. I like to go to these new restaurants and tell the waiters to bring me their favorite dishes on the menu. We ended up getting a few extra plates just to have some variety. But the food was so fantastic, we pretty much ate everything!

It was very relaxing and nice. He even walked me to my car at the end of dinner and kissed me goodbye. When I got home I saw that I had a missed call from him as I plugged my phone in. I checked my voice mail to find an actual message from him this time asking if he would see me next week. I texted him back with a smiley, confirming our date for next week. But he replied back with, '" changed my mind, that's a bit too far away. How about this Thursday?" Clearly, I am more than okay with this.

It seemed like an eternity but Thursday had finally arrived. I secretly took the entire day off from work so I could prepare for my third date with the chef. I had planned on relaxing and taking it easy today. Going out with the chef has become quite the focus of my life and I definitely needed some zen and retail therapy to be 100% ready for the night ahead. But as I was halfway down the page of my friend's latest novel while I soaked up some sun on the roof of my apartment, my phone started chirping with that familiar sound.

It was the chef. He wanted to know if I would also meet up for lunch in addition to our dinner date. Well, okay; I suppose I can make this happen. He said to meet up at 1PM, but I end up being an hour late thanks to this fucking horrendous west side traffic. I swear, in Los Angeles, if it's not one thing with the traffic it's always another. As I arrive, he already had a table waiting for us to eat on the promenade. This was a quiet and cute little place where we were able to share some salads and wine. It was nice to take a mid-day break for once. If I had been at work, there is no way I could escape long enough to enjoy something this fantastic.

We finished up our food and I excused myself to the restroom. It's a long drive back to Hollywood so it seemed logical to go now while we waited on the check. I came back to the table and he was already standing up ready to leave. I got a little flustered seeing he had already paid for the whole check secretly. How clever Mr. Chef. I made sure to let him know that I am picking up the dinner tab no matter how much he begs or pleads.

We went our separate ways, and I went home to start getting ready for the night. I didn't want to doll it up too much seeing as he has already seen sides of me most will never, so I just put on my normal pair of skinny jeans with a bit of tearing in the pocket, a low-cut black tank top and leather jacket get up.

I drove over to his house later in the evening after the traffic and heat of this city had cooled off a bit. I picked him up and took him to one of my favorite sushi spots in this city. We definitely ordered way too much food, and might have had one too many sakes. But that's more than okay. We had quite a pleasurable time laughing and enjoying each other's company. We even got lost on the drive back to his house. When we finally got back on track and got close, he told me to find some street parking and invited me up for a night cap. My mind raced faster than he could speak those words with the thought this might just finally equal sex.

He poured me one of my specialties, as he calls it, of Vodka and Sprite. It kept the buzz going good as I seductively make my way from the kitchen to his couch. He picked up on the hint rather quickly and almost like a shadow followed me to his couch. He turned on the TV and I immediately changed the channel to watch, *The Real Housewives of Atlanta*. He totally thought I was crazy, but I could see it in his eyes that he truly was entertained by this train wreck of a reality show. We cuddled for a bit, and slowly touch each other till he can't take it anymore. He climbed right on top of me and started passionately kissing me and working his way down my neck with his sexy lips. They found their way down to the cleavage on my shirt and began to tug at the shirt. He slowly used his hands to run his way up from the bottom of the shirt and massaged my breasts.

As the drunk began to settle in, the make out session led back to the bedroom. This time we really did go for it. We both seemed to have magically lost our clothes in a bout of fury and passion. As he was grinding his penis on the outside of me, I could see almost a trail of clothing leading from the couch to the bedroom as if we were an adult-rated version of Hansel and Gretel. He reached into the night stand and I could feel myself almost instantly orgasm at the thought of what is going to happen next.

He unwrapped the condom and stretches it over the tip of his rock hard cock, and shoves it inside me. Not violently like one would think, but with enough force to be dominant while being sweet. He was on top for quite some time before I took over and rode him like there was no tomorrow. My breasts bounced up and down and he had to look away because the way they moved made him want to cum. Too excited from it, he flipped me on my knees and continued to pound me in doggy style. Boy, the stamina this guy had. It seemed like we banged for a good hour in doggy before he finally gave a final thrust and let his semen fill the condom inside me.

Breathless, he rolled over next to me and looked me dead in the eye and jokingly says, "Well, that wasn't supposed to happen." I gave him a giggle to reassure him that it did. It also happened very well. We ended up falling asleep immediately after, and I woke up around 7 AM to his arms around me, conforming to my curved body. As pleasant as this was, and as much as I wanted it, it was time to go. So I maneuvered myself out of his death grip, and hunted down my clothes around his apartment and left.

I got a text a couple hours later asking why I left so soon. To be honest, I couldn't tell you why either. We still hung out a couple times after that, and kept in touch via email and text as he traveled across the country, and eventually the world with reunion shows and competitions. I like to think that we didn't really break up, but more so I just broke him in for the next girls to flock towards his innocent, shy and handsome self. Our brief encounter with dating was the perfect thing I needed after going through a rough break up two months before.

Fetishes Only Ruin Shoes

There's a rule of mine that I try to hold to as much as humanly possible when it comes to hook ups and flings, and that is to never spend the night. This has taught me a great deal of self control over the course of the years by making sure I'm sober enough to leave after sex, or at least good enough to sleep for an hour and leave. Even that is pushing it. This rule has gotten me very accustomed to walking into my apartment at four in the morning. But walking into my apartment with the gross feeling of cum between my toes at four in the morning? Well, that's a little different.

I swear every time I remember my DJ phase, I feel like I have to immediately wash my feet before the urge to vomit gets too great. The DJ phase really didn't even have time to become a phase, because the first guy I met simply ruined it all with his "Fetish."

When I mention DJs, everyone immediately thinks I was some DJ whore jumping from club to club like a drugged up groupie, banging mainstream headliners like Skrillex, or David Guetta. But when I say DJ, I don't mean that washed up 90s gutter punk who made it big by knowing how to press play just right on their Macbook Serrato set up. I mean real talent. There is nothing hotter than a guy who can drop an ass-bumping beat on pure vinyl. There's really just nothing that can compare to the way a real record smells, feels, and sounds. And it's sad watching talentless and spoiled kids make it to the top, when the real men are still stuck playing shitty warehouse parties in dangerous parts of the town. I still have a fucking fetish with DJs to this day, I will admit.

I was at a party one night, and decided to take some ecstasy. That's when I met one of the DJs named, Anthony, who actually approached me first. My pills had more than kicked in at the time and I was willing to talk to anyone about pretty much everything as long as they were willing to listen. But he didn't seem to mind. He let me put my designer purse and leather jacket behind the DJ booth next to his equipment. He played this insane Michael Jackson mashup that had everyone dancing their asses off. When I am rolling on ecstasy, I prefer the company of a wall to dance against like in the music videos that MTV used to play. Hot girls dancing and leaning against the wall of the club, yeah that's me. He ended up giving me his number and borderline begging me to text him right in front of him. If I wasn't so hopped up on MDMA, I might have been a bit smarter than his played out game.

Within a week of texting, we had already become well acquainted. Not only had I experienced the good parts of drinking two bottles of champagne while he played me a special mix, and smoking weed until the sun rose through the smog of this congested city, but I had also seen plenty of the bad.

I frankly don't even know how to start with what went wrong, especially with the sudden dramatic turn it took.

The easiest of ways to explain this would have to be by me pretending to be a naughty teacher, reading you the cliff notes, and you being my pervy student. Please think about my long legs in a short, plaid mini skirt and white button-down shirt as I point to a chalkboard and read the following:

1.   Never invite a woman over to watch *Family Guy*. No matter how hot you are it only speaks to how retarded you are.

2.   Matching sheets. If you want to have sex with the lights on, matching sheets. And not one of those ugly WalMart bed-in-a-bag comforter sets.

3.   A little bit of oral goes a long way.

4.   It's nice when you're hung, but know how to use it.

He broke nearly every standard on this above list, but every woman has a weakness. And mine at the time just so happened to be everything he was involved in..

I decided to go over to his house one night, after he clearly broke rule number 1 on my list. After a bottle of wine, I was on his level of mental retardation and ready to face the bedroom. This is where rule number 2 was broken. His whole apartment was comprised of mismatched furniture, most of which looked like he got it in the free section of Craigslist. And his bed definitely was a clearance bed-in-a-bag item because the color schemes could not have been better chosen by Helen Keller.

Rule number 3 was easily broken the minute he pushed me on the bed, and tried to jam his 10 inches of man inside of me raw and dry. I'm not one to say no to a lot of things, but when someone is a bit of a celebrity within a smaller group of individuals, I am going to assume you sleep around. And your unprotected man meat isn't coming anywhere near my temple without an STD check, or a condom.

After he put the condom on, while nearly throwing a temper tantrum in the process, I spent the better part of twenty minutes lying there and having my pussy beaten with a ten-inch disco stick. It was becoming a bit too much and he was looking rather foolish and too far from finishing. I couldn't even take this seriously at this point so I decided to curl up my leg around him and suck on my foot as he continued to pound my vagina like an obese, American butcher.

"You like that mama?" he said to me in between slurps of my toes. Or at least I'm pretty sure that's what I heard.

Really? No.

Finally he pulled out and ripped the condom off so he could give me his grand finale... all over my feet. The same feet that had to go back into an eight hundred dollar pair of shoes; leaving me with some serious things to think about after I took a nap. But I'd be damned if I broke my own rule of spending the night at this asshole's house. So instead that nap would have to be briefly scheduled in during the three pedicures I now had lined up thanks to this disgusting glob of baby gravy covering my perfect french tip.

The last thing that I wanted to hear, is of course the first thing to come out of his mouth. How typical. He genuinely wants to know when he can give me my next foot massage.

Is the answer, "How about never?" okay to use in this situation? Well, I really didn't need your permission to blurt that one out immediately. And this is why I day drink.

Oh Anthony, if only I were still foggy on ecstasy like the night I met you, then maybe I wouldn't mind the sticky feeling you left between my toes.

And I Thought a Guy Cumming on My Feet Was Weird

It was your average night in Los Angeles, and by average I mean the normal busybody Hollywood events filled with your less-than-average celebrities and wannabes. These types of gatherings never really tickled my fancy, so I opted out for the remainder of the evening to sip my Vodka from the open bar quietly on a stoop out front when he arrived.

He stepped out of his vehicle and rose up to what had to have been well over six feet tall. Even in my stilettos, he had to have been almost a good foot taller than me, if not more. He made brief eye contact as he walked directly past me without saying a word. In my experience at these events, never once had I encountered someone who could simply ignore my existence as he did especially when I was wearing my lucky red dress. Was he straight? Clearly not if he couldn't even give me a simple hello, or a smile from what I know had to be perfectly whitened veneers behind those luscious lips. Was he married and just chose to ignore me out of his fear of temptation? I found it just far too strange, and made it my mission for the night to figure out what his deal was.

I quickly threw the remainder of my cigarette into the street and finished the last few drops of Vodka from my cup as I quickly made my way back into the building. My liquid courage had my adrenaline pumping over time, and before I knew it, I had fully marched up to him and managed to introduce myself. Confidence had never really been an issue for me, but whenever I had a little to drink my body was always 10 steps ahead of my brain. Before long, Mr. Tall, Dark and Handsome and I had quite the conversation going. Turns out he was a Football player for some NFL team or another. I have never been one to be into sports, so the name really never stuck with me. But his name did, and boy did he have a name as stunning as he was…Schuylar.

I looked down at my watch and noticed that an hour and a half had already passed since Schuylar and I had started talking. Flirting, laughing, and just a great conversation was all it took for me to see something special in him. Butterflies were stirring in my stomach at the thought of his perfectly carved jaw along my inner thigh, Maybe it was the drinks starting to add up, but I suddenly had a thought cross my mind that we hadn't discussed yet. How old is he?

Schuylar's response was quite unsettling when I came to realize that he was only 24. Being four years older than him, I suddenly felt a bit off. I started to see the maturity levels between us as quite polar opposites. My intellect was quite on par with where it should be for my age, if not a bit more advanced. While the conversational level from him tended to be a bit more one-sided and stuck in High School mode. But age had never stopped me from obtaining anyone's number in the past, and it certainly wasn't going to hold me back tonight.

We parted ways that night but I woke up the next morning to a text from Schuylar containing a photo of his marble carved body and chiseled abs lying across the bed. At the end of the message, it played the sound of his crisp, smooth voice saying, "Good Morning Beautiful." While it did make me smile for a few seconds, it was totally not my style. But to give him the benefit of the doubt, he was only 24.

The texting of one worded answers and sentences quickly picked back up into a full conversation, similar to the night before. Then suddenly he asked me, 'Have you ever had a threesome with two dudes?" My instant response back to him was a sharp, and all-capped, "FUCK NO!" Without even trying to persuade me into doing it, he went back to a simple conversation. But almost every hour on the hour my phone would receive another sexual and almost interrogative question from Schuylar. It was cute the first few times, but this went on for roughly four days until I decided that we should meet up.

He didn't understand at first why I wouldn't invite him over. Hell, sometimes I don't even get why I would rather fuck in a hotel room than in my own bed. And don't even get me started as to what my therapist has said about it, because it has been a whole lot of stuttering, babbling, and confusion with her from the start. Sometimes, it's as if I pay her just to listen while I figure out my own way to go about things. Oh, and of course, the pills.

At first I thought it would be some shitty, run-down beach motel, and when I showed up my idea of where I would end up wasn't far off from that. But when I got into the room he had surprised me with a fancy bottle of champagne to break the ice. It was the thought that counted with Schuylar, and I felt like I should take what I could get from him because it seemed he didn't have many thoughts to give.

To put it out there let me just tell you I have never once or ever will be what I like to refer to as a, "Jersey Chaser." And if I wasn't clear enough by that idea let me just set you straight by saying I do not fuck athletes. But everyone has their exceptions. Mine just happened to be a walking billboard for the Jolly Green Giant undercover Football Player.

Imagine every Hollywood cliché hook up you have ever visually enjoyed on a late night soft core cable porno. Now take away the fancy hotel, and add two highly attractive individuals instead of your average run of the mill B-movie actors. That would perfectly describe what was about to happen.

The sun was setting outside and peeking its farewell rays in between the drapes. He slowly pulled off my top and simultaneously threw me down onto the bed. Pulling off my shorts with his rough hands, he kissed his way up my thigh and pulled my underwear down with his teeth. He slowly undressed me with his mouth and made his way around every curve of my body that the sunset was still touching. His masculine body dominated mine as he started to get on top. He quickly undressed himself and revealed what I had long been waiting to see, his giant, rock-hard penis. It was just as beautiful as the rest of him. And the minute it thrust into me, he started to whisper the dirtiest of things into my ear; and not in the good way either.

I love dirty talk with a passion but there are certain rules to be followed when engaging in it. I like to put it into 3 simple topics.

1. What I'm going to do to you

2. What I am doing to you

3. What I did to you

When you stick to these 3 key ideas, there isn't much that can go wrong, and there is so much to go right. But when I say Schuylar was a nasty, dirty boy in the sheets, I mean it. Never once have I heard such filthy and borderline repulsive things come from such a perfect looking mouth.

Halfway through Schuylar screamed out in a fit of passion, "'Your pussy is so tight and wet I want to watch my whole team fuck it." Caught off guard, I let out a drawn out "umm" before giving him that cross look between "What the fuck?" and "No". For as dumb as he was, he quickly caught on and went back to being dominate without so much of the speech.

After what seemed like an eternity of pure, raw, aggressive sex, the grand finale occurred. He rolled over to the side of me as we both gasped for air. Exhausted and feeling rejuvenated, I reached over for a cigarette from the nightstand but I don't think I even made it to the pack before passing out.

The next thing I knew, I woke up to a darkened room and the feeling of him between my thighs. There is nothing hotter than being woken up to a guy you are being intimate with going down on you, especially at 4 in the morning. We had slept straight through dinner, and I could have slept straight through lunch if he wasn't waking me up for his kinky version of breakfast.

As he got me going, I decided it was my turn to have a little fun. I repositioned myself so I could quickly get on top of him to work my way down to his cock. But as I tried to transfer my body to on top of him, he suddenly blurted out, 'Would you mind fingering my ass as I jack off?'

It's as if I was doing 85mph in a 45 mph zone and suddenly a young kid runs out in front of my vehicle. All the brakes within my brain were working overtime so I could comprehend what he just said. I couldn't tell if he was this freaky, or if he almost had a case of erotic turrets.

Even though it was something I wasn't into at all, the accommodating and experimental side of me agreed to it. I kissed his inner thighs and even put my lips around his dick as he slowly rubbed his hand up and down the shaft. But it wasn't enough for him and asked me if I would be willing to use my tongue to pleasure his hole.

My brain pleaded, "No, no, no!" but my mouth agreed to at least try it once. And so I made my way to the back side of him and slowly kissed his cheeks apart. I tried to do it, and get passed all the gross and childish thoughts running through my head, but I just couldn't bring myself to doing it on a level where he would enjoy it and shortly after stopped.

I mean, it's 4 AM. Can't we just have normal sex so I can get myself back to my beauty sleep? But my inner thighs were still so sore from riding him, and being ridden into the ground, that it was even a complicated idea to fathom his humongous cock inside of me. I completely did the girl move with a quick yawn to show that I am tired and would rather sleep instead of engaging with him. He ended up giving me a virgin-like attitude with, "Fine, if you won't help me I'll do it myself."

I shrugged it off and said whatever, in my head of course. I rolled over and pulled the covers back on as he sat upright on the edge of the bed still tugging on his shaft and fingering his own ass. Luckily this didn't last for long since he had to leave at 8am for a training and conditioning session. He kissed me goodbye and was gone. I was so fucking happy because I could still sleep for two more hours in peace without worrying about being woken up by anal fantasies. I took my time getting ready and left for work and couldn't wait to tell my gay best friend Reilly this story from last night.

Tweet Tweet Tyler

With the rise of social media outlets in the past decade, it's no wonder why online dating has become such a big success especially with the ease of hiding ones identity with conveniently angled photos and the ways to mask one's true self by committing a less severe version of identity fraud.

With social media outlets like Myspace and Facebook where you have to create a profile, spend countless hours perfecting every little detail about it through photographs, layouts, video uploads, etc. it was only a matter of time until til something grabbed my eye that was simpler. And in 2009, I had gotten my wish with Twitter.

Even though I joined in 2009, it wasn't until around 2011 when I became an active "tweeter". And by that I mean I was joining trending topics, creating them, and even lurking and tweeting new people who seemed to meet my interests. But never really did I stop and think that online dating would make its way into something like this. On Twitter, each message has to be 140 characters or less even when you go into talking to users through DMs (which is like a private chat). So even trying to get across a telephone number with an address can leave you abbreviating most words like you caught a case of Internet Ebonics.

The first guy I met through Twitter was a man named Tyler. He was vacationing on some exotic island far away enough to catch my eye and make me quite green with envy. He sent me on of those DM's and started up a casual yet flirty conversation with me. Of course, before I could reply back I had to do some of my investigating and stalk his profile to see if he was even real, or worth my time. I looked on his profile until I came down to the last of his tweets. He was a 24, Santa Monica prep boy, with the stereotypical Abercrombie look to go with it. His Twitter account had been around for quite enough time for me to take the bait and send him back a couple "winkies" over the course of the next few days. After a week of talking, we agreed to meet back up when he got back into the states. But to put my mind on ease, I also added him on Facebook to find out a little bit more about him and to see who I'm truly dealing with.

As the notification popped up saying he accepted my friend request on Facebook, I got the little girly butterflies in my stomach. Not the kind that tell me I'm in love, but the kind you get right before you know you're going to get laid. I started browsing his photos and he definitely fits the Abercrombie mold even more than I thought. Most of them are him and his buddies out at the club with shitty frat boy beer in their hands and some cheap lasers behind them with probably a resident DJ running the same played out club hits from last month. But I'll give him the benefit of the doubt for being 24. I mean, who wasn't all crazy, wet and wild at that age? I don't even want to get started on the wild things I did at 24. The rest of the photos were him with who looked like his ex-girlfriend and a whole album dedicated to his two bulldogs. They weren't the normal show off styled photos of bulldogs, but I could see he had a genuine soft spot for animals. Swoon!

It seemed like an eternity until he finally tweeted me saying he was going to be landing at LAX in a couple days. Hell, it had been so long I had almost actually moved on to some fresh meat I had lined up. His idea of a perfect evening involved wine and a movie at his place. Even as pretentious as that sounds, it was actually quite enjoyable.

I slipped on my favorite skinny jeans with just the right amount of tear along the legs to give him a hint of what's to come, along with my favorite platform booties. To spice it up, I kept it simple with a white tank to show off the right amount of cleavage with my new Victoria Secret bra. But Santa Monica gets too cold in the evening for a tank top no matter what time of the year it is so I put the finishing touches on the outfit with my rock star-esque leather jacket. The funny thing is this outfit is what most women wear when they want to go out to the club, but this was just my normal casual get up. Nothing makes your ass look better than a tight pair of jeans.

With rush hour traffic working against me, I finally arrived to his house 20 minutes late. I should be used to these fancy guys I meet who have nice places on the coast, but time and time again my jaw drops when I walk into an apartment that is identical to last month's Ikea catalog especially when it has the perfect view of the California sunset. To get into his building I had to deal with more security than most of the high profile celebrities I have met and hung out with in my day. I even had an elevator escort take me to the top floor and make sure I went the right way. This totally gave me the wrong idea. I mean the guy is 24 and somewhat of an entrepreneur, and living well for someone his age. What if he totally misrepresented himself?

He answered the door with a heartwarming smile, and I was instantly knocked over by his two bulldogs. Slobbery, wet drool made its way all over my favorite shoes; perfect. Tyler told me not to mind them and said that he will have my shoes cleaned while we hang out. I insisted that it wasn't necessary but he was quite the persistent type. As I unzipped the back of my shoes I couldn't help but think, "Well, that's one less thing to take off later."

He sent the shoes down to be cleaned by the on-site staff and then tried to reintroduce himself. "Sorry about that; sometimes these big boys like to steal the spotlight." He took my hand and led me into the kitchen and asked me to close my eyes. I'm not one to do what strangers ask in their home, but I felt okay abiding by this one statement as it sounded like a fun game in the making. I closed my eyes then he asked me to point my hand anywhere along the wall. When my hand stopped I opened my eyes and had chosen a bottle of red wine that was well worth a couple grand. He popped it open like it was a bottle of Two Buck Chuck, almost as a way to impress me with his extravagant lifestyle. Needless to say, I was completely falling for his wallet. I'm definitely not a gold digger, but no one can resist the charm and suaveness of what someone who is significantly younger than you and easily making your yearly salary in a matter of months can provide. In the words of our Twitter generation, he definitely had swag.

We made our way back to the living room and I had his two bulldogs shadowing me with every step. They were quite fond of me, even Tyler had some commentary about how he had never seen them so attached to someone so quickly. Quite cute, but let's not forget the real reason I was here... to hook up casually. And nothing more.

Unfortunately, he didn't have the perfect movie to compliment the worth of this wine. He had picked out some shitty sequel of an action movie that couldn't have broken even with box office sales. But in my eyes, every movie is great when you have more than enough alcohol.

Because I am on the tiny side, it doesn't take long for me to get a nice wine buzz going on. And that's my queue to initiate the signal. I lifted my feet up onto the couch underneath my body, but ever so slightly pointed to the side as if I could lean into him. This is always the number one hint to guys that we want a move to be made. He took the bait and scooted over a bit so I could rest my head ever so lightly on his marble carved shoulder, but I had slight confusion when it came to that. Was I supposed to make the first move because I was older? Or was it still his job as a gentleman to make it?

His arm draped over my leg for quite some time. I didn't feel like I was going to grow impatient, but I was actually starting to get into this movie, whatever it was. But just as I had started to give up hope on him, he leaned in for the kiss and finally made the move. Nicely played

Twitter boy. The kiss was fantastic. One of those that you could imagine having on New Year's in a different country as fireworks go off and thousands and thousands, maybe millions people cheer off in the distance. It quickly escalated into dry humping on his couch and with a swift motion he picked me up and carried me to the bedroom. Impressive he did all of that without missing a moment of the kissing.

He gently lay me down on the bed and the clothes began to rip off, almost like we secretly had the super powers of the incredible hulk. His hands made their way up and down my entire body, caressing every inch and curve of it. Just touching and making out wasn't enough for me though. I wanted some more fun with the foreplay and to bring some oral into it. But the only oral he wanted was his tongue in my mouth, unfortunately.

It was the cookie cutter sex positioning of him starting on top, than turning me onto my stomach for a backwards missionary-esque position. That led to me riding his cock for quite some time until he couldn't take it any longer and just had to cum. On a scale of 1-10, I'd give it a solid 6. I didn't orgasm, and obviously that was due to the lack of foreplay. It wasn't quite exciting either. There's one thing I can't stand in the bedroom is selfish lovers. But his hot model type body and his beautiful, almost statue like cock gave him a couple extra points.

As he finished, he lay down next to me almost as if he was expecting me to say something. I just rolled over to face him and smiled, while giving out a cute little yawn.

But that yawn quickly turned into the real thing with my wine drunk going on.

I woke up around 4 AM with an insane urge to use the bathroom. And there I was, lying naked in his bed with one of the bulldogs creating a wall between us. And as I got ready to position myself to stand up with my butt on the edge of his bed, I nearly stepped on the other sleeping at the foot of it. Slightly irritated and still quite inebriated, I decided it would be a great idea to attempt to lift this 60-something pound bulldog off the ground and into the bed. During my attempt I accidentally woke up Tyler, and he politely offered to get the dog for me, but I insisted to do it on my own. He rolled back over and immediately fell asleep.

It took a little too long but finally the dog was willing to cooperate and got into the bed. And at that point I had lost my second wind and decided sleep sounded good for another few hours. So there I was, still naked, lying in bed next to two slobbery, yet so beautiful and sweet bulldogs. I woke up again to the bright sunshine poking its head through the window along with Tyler's snoring. I checked my phone and saw that it was 9:30 AM and decided now was the best time to sneak out if I didn't want to get caught and forced into him making me breakfast or something.

Don't get me wrong, Tyler was an amazing guy. And we still both follow each other on Twitter and chat all the time. But he just really wasn't my type. A casual hook up from time to time was okay, but it seemed like there would be too much too fast and that always spells disaster with the caps lock on.

Tweeter in My Twat

Speaking of the idea of Twitter and casual encounters, I think it genuinely freaks guys out when they realize we actually live in the same city and all this playful banter has a chance of moving from behind the computer to a real life connection. But in my experience, telling someone you are from Los Angeles, is almost like telling someone else, "I'm from North America too!" especially if you live on opposite sides of the coast.

Los Angeles is such a large, and diverse city that even if you live there, you can still be an hour away from its opposite side on a good day when there is no traffic, construction, celebrity events and award shows, or random presidential visits going on in the town.

Like most internet flings, it always starts off with the tweeting back and forth…playfully, flirty, and sometimes down and dirty. If I could write a chart that would describe the way Twitter hook ups work, it would start off with tweeting for roughly a week, then the idea of exchanging numbers and texting back and forth for the next month or so. Then when there is a level of comfortability and trust, meeting in the flesh will occur.

And this is how it has happened time and time again, and especially how it happened with Patrick. If I could describe Patrick in five words or less, I would only need three to say he was young, attractive and green. He was new to Los Angeles, but his genuine care for everything around him wasn't an act or facade like all the other LA men. He brought a beautiful smile and positive attitude to everything he did. He was probably one of the few I had met in a really long time that actually had not repulsed me by their hypocrisy on first sight.

It was 8 PM and Santa Monica was just starting to cool off after a long hot day. We met up at a local pub with no real expectations except to get drunk and have some fun. When he first walked in, I thought it was almost a joke. His cute khaki pants and a blue sweater made him look too prim and proper for a woman like myself. But who am I to judge?

I knew it was him as he walked in by his smile. I mean, even though I had seen countless photos of him on Twitter, it was the way his smile illuminated the room that made me know for sure it was him. He didn't even bother trying to introduce himself when he walked up to me which was quite pleasant. I mean we had talked so much over the past couple of weeks that an introduction really wasn't needed. His voice was overly pleasant and soothing. I could easily pay him to do voiceovers on my favorite books just so I had a reason to listen to his voice all day.

We walked over to an empty table in the back so we could have a chance at hearing one another over the loud drunks sitting near the bar. Pint after pint kept making their way back to us and the conversation started to become quite eccentric and all over the map. We discussed everything from childhood, to my ex stripper days, and I'm not too sure, but I even think there might have been some college sports talk at some point. Yes, random, I know.

After my third beer, we decided it was time for us to part ways so I could start my drive back to Hollywood. Patrick offered to walk me to my car but I wasn't too sure about that. I mean, even though I just spent the better part of the night talking to him, it was just something I felt safer not allowing. But he managed to convince me to walk me halfway to my car. After getting a block away from the bar, I stopped him at the crosswalk and said, '"Well, I'm close enough."

He leaned his body up against a wall and pulled me in for a kiss. For such a dramatic maneuver I expected more of a spark or something. But there was little to nothing going off in my stomach, heart or head at this point. But it was very romantic and soft and overall a nice kiss.

I turned off and walked to my car, with each step inhaling the fresh scent of ocean in the night breeze. I couldn't help but think to myself the whole drive back to my house that he was a really nice guy, but I will fucking tear him apart harder than *She Wants Revenge* could ever with that hit song.

Patrick and I continued to text back and forth daily over the next week. And, I couldn't say no when he asked me out on a date to one of my favorite spots in Culver City that Friday. I chose a sheer black top with a leopard bra underneath. Sexy and youthful, yet enough coverage to keep away from giving him the wrong ideas about this.

We met up and he was looking stunningly handsome in just something as simple as jeans and a sweater. And once again, I look like a rented high-end escort next to his innocence.

The best part about it was that his energy and positivity was the same as I remembered. It wasn't a front just to get in my pants like most guys, and it was very appreciated. We shared a nice bottle of wine while we talked about the past week and its ventures. I felt bad for spacing out while he talked, but I was off in another world wondering what sex would actually be like with someone so different from "my type."

After a lovely meal and non-stop chatter, I decided that we should take the conversation down the street to one of my favorite late night bars in the local hotel. As we stepped inside the radio was blasting Adele's hit train wreck, '"Rolling in the Deep." God I hate that song. So depressing. So overplayed.

I suggested we sit outside due to the awkward music inside. We ordered two glasses of my favorite Pinot Noir and continued our talk as we made commentary to the passer bys. It's always funny how life throws you these curve balls that seem to be exactly what you needed. While I wasn't in need of what he was searching for when it came to a woman, I liked the aspect of being his friend. It was pleasant.

As the wine began to catch up to the both of us, and rather quickly, we decided it would be fun to drive all the way back to his place in Santa Monica and continue our drinking session there. Not the wisest decision I had made in a while, but we'll just let it slide for now.

Another glass of Pinot Noir and 30 minutes later I found myself in a parking garage on the far west side. It's an awkward moment when you realize you have parked in this same garage more times than you can remember in the past few years. And they all revolve around the same reason.

It seemed like the night was going good. I walked up into his condo with him by my side. Modern, clean and extremely minimalistic with everything lined with chrome. Chrome fridge, chrome sink, hell, even the furniture had chrome somehow built into the frame. Very much a "boy's pad" but clean which is always appreciated. He grabbed another bottle of wine from the fridge and gave me an apologetic smile when he told me the only thing he had to drink it from were what looked like Target Margarita glasses. At this point I didn't even care. Just let me at it already.

We made it into the bedroom as he dimmed the lights and we started to cuddle and continued our talk. The wine caught up far too quickly, and I dropped my entire glass on his white comforter set. Oops! He said it wasn't a big deal and I even offered to replace it at this point. In his exact words, he said, "Don't worry about it. I'll go buy a new comforter and sheet set tomorrow before my date with.."

I didn't catch her name. I began to build with a bit of rage the minute he said date. It wasn't out of jealousy, or actually wanting to be exclusive with him. He was too nice and we had no physical connection whatsoever with the smallest kiss.

My liquor mouth got the best of me as I started to attack him with vicious remarks. And most of which are completely valid. I don't date younger men for this exact reason. They think they can date multiple partners at the same time like some sick, unscripted version of the bachelor until they find their one. Then they cut the strings with all the others eventually. Now, I didn't feel so bad for accidentally cock-blocking him with my wine spill.

Even though I had picked a fight with someone I had only met twice at this point, I wasn't going to leave empty handed. Things calmed down with his swift apology, and I just let it slide knowing this was the last time I'd make an effort to talk to him. He used kissing on my neck while he said he was sorry, and worked his way down to my chest, pulling down the neck of my shirt to get deeper.

I didn't even want it at this point, but I was still a bit too drunk to make my way on home and escape. So I said fuck it, and let him continue, thinking I was going to get mine. But his lack of an erection (lets blame the wine on this one) made the sex... well... pointless. This was just pathetic. What a waste of my time, my evening... my life. I could be out there with dozens of other guys, yet I chose hanging out with someone who had presented himself to me as a nice guy. The truth is he was a nice guy. He made me smile and turned my bad girl mage inside out. But he needed to work on his drinking so that he can show me that cock of his when its fully erect.

Patrick and I are still friends in real life and on Twitter of course. He will probably always be in my life and as long as we can both laugh about that night, we may have a lifelong friendship on our hands. And if you're reading this Patrick… advice to you…always stay two glasses of wine behind me. xoxo

The Freaks of the Free Online Weekend (Online Emails)

Welcome to the inbox of an actual hot woman who online dates in this, the city of fallen angels.

"Hey there!
I'm 4'11", 73 pounds overweight, I've got super long hair- like past my shoulders- and tattoos all over my body. I'm 68 years old and just got my 7th body piercing this past weekend. Sound good so far? Just kidding!
I saw your profile and I think you deserve a chance to get to know me. If you sound as interesting as your profile says, I might write you back. ;) "
*Seriously, I deserve to know you? You deserve a case of herpes and my block button.

"I just read your profile and it's very well written I'm John what's ur name?
Perhaps we could talk whenever u feel comfortable?
I was married for 20 years and was faithful. New to dating online. Just new to dating period.
I'm 38 yrs old and have a great career in aerospace manufacturing.
U never know what people God will cross ur path with. Everything happens for a reason. Good or bad."

* I don't even know where to start with you. So let's start with "u" and "ur". You email like a 14-year-old girl who hasn't had her period yet. No wonder your wife left you. But props on being faithful for twenty years, I'm pretty

sure your wife wasn't.

"Hi,
No sales pitch. I like you... Interested in me?"
Dan"

*Two words: Hell No.

"Hi,
I like to keep things simple and sweet so here I go...I find
you very cute and adorable, and liked what you had to
say in your profile. It seems like you have your life in
order and I would really like the opportunity to meet you.
A nice hike would be super duper, but since we don't
know each other I'm good with meeting for coffee, tea, or
maybe even breakfast lunch or dinner! I want you to feel
comfy so let me know how you would like to proceed. You
may also Yelp my business or better yet go to my website.
Sincerely,
Nandor
Ps. Here's my number just in case (310) xxx-xxxx"

* The fact that you used the term super duper is
borderline creepy but kind of amazing at the same time.
What part of my online profile says that I enjoy hiking?
My profile is brief and focuses on my main interests:
booze and expensive meals. And no, I will not log onto
Yelp and search for our shitty personal training business
that leaves you with a huge beer gut.

"Happy Sunday!
How's a nice boy like me get you to Manhattan
Beach/Santa Monica next weekend for a pre Valentines
Day martini? Hmmm... Well I tried to keep my extremely
lame message short, to the point and not too creepy
unlike the other 750 emails I'm sure you got last week.
Chris"

*Your tag line is "I'm a boss" located underneath your
lame flexing profile photo is "Manhattan Beach's Most
Eligible Bachelor 2007". It looks like you'll be eligible a
lot longer.

"WOW, WOW gorgeous eyes!!!!!!!!!
That is my weakness!!!!!!!
Wanted to say hello!!!!!
Anthony!!!!"

* Hey Anthony, slow down with your exclamation
points.

"Hi, is the guy in your pictures you have posted your
boyfriend?"

*That guy you're referring to in my photos is my best
friend. He just happens to have a penis that is attracted to
other men. Get a fucking life, "beefpatty11"? I'd ask you
what type of username that is but I fear further contact

from you.

"Question... How did you get so pretty?
Rob"

Sigh Rob, honey. It's not me. It's you. You're listed as sober. I can't have that in life.

"I know you dream of...
Being taken out by a charismatic, fun, fit, too sexy for his hair, articulate, successful and hilarious entertainment attorney! Don't deny it! Have a great weekend.
Scott"

* Have you looked in the mirror? What you typed makes zero sense.

"Hi,
Your profile caught my attention, two dogs? Well you must not be too wild or irresponsible if the dogs are still kicking. Gold star.
I hope that picture is really you and you're not some old guy sitting in a basement petting a chicken.
I moved here 4 years ago from NY after getting my masters at Columbia. I am a writer, mostly comedy.
I hope you're as cool as your profile makes you out to be. I've got some questions for you.
Michael"

*I haven't received a gold star since 2nd grade. Petting a

chicken in my basement?

Subject: Boy looking for a mommy
"*Lexa,*
You tame and wild person. Tame and wild...makes
perfect sense by the way.
In all seriousness, I'm planning on robbing a bank
tonight and thought you'd be great at driving the getaway
car. No chance of getting caught...we will drive off the
pier in Santa Monica and fake our own deaths. And don't
worry, I have scuba gear in the back just bring a change
of clothes and out them in a water proof bag for gods
sake.
Chris
PS. bring snacks...might get hungry. I say egg salad
sandwiches!"

* You had me at egg salad sandwiches.
God one day into this free weekend trail and I'm already
deleting my profile.

When Will I Learn? (Online Dating Emails)

More online dating *WTF's*. The more we know right?

"Hi ;-)
I like your profile! You a Organ State Beaver? Are you
from Organ? If so what brought you to LA? I'd love to
chat and learn more!
;-) Travis"

* Jackass, learn to spell and you're 38, stop using fucking wink face emoticons.

"Hi,
Beautiful Asian lovely u are"

* How much more creepy can you be? Rape much?

"I think you'd be someone that I could get along well with
I like a lot of the things you mentioned...
Give me a shout and we can start a life and adventure
together.
Cheers, Peter"

*You're 42, Asian, overweight. The only adventure you should start is with a treadmill.

"Haha I remember you! Ha! Hey! I think we met a few years back on and briefly met at Foxtails. It's Ryan. I may be mistaken, but your facebook profile picture was Plexico Burress right after he shot himself, priceless. How's life?"

* I have never even been to Foxtails and I had to Google who Plexico Burress was. Stop going to strip clubs.

"YOU LOOK SOOOOOOOOOOO CUTE! HIIIIIIIIIIIIIIII, I wish y r fine, my name is Timmo living in Torrance, CA and working in Dubai as branch manager for a food stuff co. I went through ur profile and i like it and i wish to know more about u and to c u soon. I will be glad if u text me on 336-xxx-xxx especially since my notebook is not working properly

Awaiting your sweet text soon,
Take care,
Timmo"

*The best line is "awaiting ur sweet text soon". The rest screams forcible anal and I'm not sixteen anymore. Blocked.

"Hello I'm James,

Hello there, how are you? I'm guessing you are Lexa. I'm James; moved here from London about a year and a half ago, really enjoy it here. So where in LA do you live? I'm in Marina Del Rey. have you been to England? anyway, I liked your profile and you look lovely in your photos. I work in El Segundo in the travel industry and I recently got my green card, so quite settled and can rest assure I'm not looking for a marriage of convenience ;) I went horse riding today. I go most Sundays up in the Santa Monica Mountains. Perhaps you'd be interested in finding out more and having a chat? hope you are having a good weekend, let me know if you would like to swap numbers.
James"

* Thank you for the intimate details of your life. The only thing you left out was your shoe size and your favorite color. Also, I should probably try and have you deported, but congrats on your Green Card and good luck finding love you freak.

"Hello :)
How are you? You have a nice smile :)

please let me take a moment and introduce myself. My name is Scott and I am originally from Buffalo, NY. yes, that is Buffalo, NY, the home of the blizzard. I also lived in Philadelphia for a few years as well before moving to LA in 1998.

I am an architect and I work in a small office that specializes in private school design. the office affords me the opportunity to design and I am grateful for that.

My interests include art, particularly modern art, architecture, history and music. My musical taste is pretty eclectic ranging from Radiohead, Beck the Flaming Lips and the Smiths to the Beatles, Pink Floyd, Public Enemy and Nick Drake.

I am also pretty athletic and like to work out 4-6 times per week.

My favorite cousin is Japanese!

I look forward to hearing from you,
Scott"

*Okay first of all, I thought Dairy Queen was the home of the blizzard, but that's just me, I guess? And congrats on your favorite cousin being Japanese. I hope you find happiness with her you cousin fucking weirdo.

.